Dedication

To all the children who believe in
always find wonder in every tale and disc
And to the storytellers who pass down
book is for you. Thank you for reminding us that our differences make the world a more colorful and meaningful place.

Lena and the Magic of Many Stories

Diversity and Inclusion

Briar Windbourne

Published by The Good Child Bookstore, 2024.

LENA AND THE MAGIC OF MANY STORIES

First edition. October 22, 2024.

ISBN: 979-8227533685

Written by Briar Windbourne.

Table of Contents

Preface

Stories have always been a window to the world, offering us glimpses of lands far away, introducing us to heroes and heroines who look different, think differently, and live differently. *Lena and the Magic of Many Stories* was inspired by the belief that through stories, children can learn the true value of diversity, equality, and inclusion. I wanted to take young readers on a journey with Lena, showing them that every story—whether from a bustling city, a quiet village, or a hidden forest—holds a piece of wisdom waiting to be discovered. My hope is that this book will spark a lifelong love for learning, exploration, and empathy in every child who reads it.

Chapter 1: The Village of One Story

In the small village of Eldena, nestled between two tall mountains and surrounded by fields of golden wheat, life moved at a peaceful, predictable pace. The houses were made of wood and stone, their roofs thatched with straw, and the people who lived there had known each other for generations. There were only about a hundred villagers, and everyone had a role to play—some were farmers, others bakers, blacksmiths, or weavers—but one thing they all shared was a single story.

This story had been passed down from parent to child, grandparent to grandchild, for as long as anyone could remember. The elders told the story on cold winter nights when the fire crackled in the hearth, and they told it on warm summer evenings when the stars twinkled in the sky. It was the same story every time, and the villagers found comfort in its familiarity. They could all recite it by heart, and it was the only story they ever told.

Lena, a curious girl of ten, had heard the story hundreds of times. She knew it so well that she could tell it even when she was half asleep. It was about a brave young man named Torin, who lived long ago in their village. Torin had fought a great battle against a fierce storm that threatened to destroy the village, and through his strength and courage, he had saved everyone. The villagers celebrated Torin's bravery every year with a festival, where they would gather in the village square, sing songs, and, of course, retell the story.

Lena loved the festival. She loved the food, the dancing, and the laughter that filled the air. But as she grew older, something began to stir inside her. While she enjoyed the story of Torin, she couldn't shake the feeling that there must be more stories out there. What about the people who lived beyond the mountains? What kinds of adventures did they have? Were their stories different? Did their heroes look like Torin, or were they different, too?

One evening, after the annual festival had come to an end and the villagers were beginning to return to their homes, Lena asked her mother a question that had been brewing in her mind for a long time.

"Mother," Lena began hesitantly, "why do we only tell the story of Torin?"

Her mother looked at her with a kind but puzzled expression. "Because, my dear, it is the story of our village. It's who we are."

"But," Lena continued, "what if there are other stories? Stories from other places, with other heroes? Wouldn't it be exciting to hear them?"

Her mother smiled gently. "Lena, our story is enough. It has always been enough. Torin was brave and strong, and his story teaches us about courage. What more do we need?"

Lena nodded, but the answer didn't satisfy her. She wanted to know more, to hear more. There was a whole world beyond the mountains, but all they ever talked about was Torin. Was it possible that the other stories her heart longed for didn't exist?

As the days passed, Lena's curiosity only grew stronger. She began to spend more time by the village's edge, gazing at the mountains and wondering what lay beyond them. She imagined all sorts of different people and places—some with sandy deserts, others with tall forests or sparkling seas. She dreamed of meeting people who spoke in languages she didn't know, of seeing animals she had only read about in old books. And most of all, she dreamed of hearing stories—new stories, full of wonders she couldn't yet imagine.

Then, one crisp autumn afternoon, something extraordinary happened.

Lena was sitting under the large oak tree at the village's edge, lost in her thoughts, when she heard the sound of hooves clattering against the cobblestones of the village road. She looked up and saw a figure approaching on a horse. It was a stranger—something that rarely happened in their small, isolated village. The man was dressed in colorful clothes, unlike anything Lena had seen before. His cloak was woven with intricate patterns of red, gold, and green, and a wide-brimmed hat shaded his face from the setting sun.

The villagers gathered quickly as the man entered the square. He dismounted from his horse and looked around with a kind smile. There was something about him that made Lena's heart race with excitement. She had never seen anyone like him, and she had a feeling that this stranger was about to change everything.

"Good evening," the man said in a deep, melodious voice that carried across the square. "I am a storyteller, a traveler from far-off lands. I bring with me tales from the four corners of the world—stories of heroes and heroines, of brave deeds and wondrous adventures."

The villagers exchanged glances, unsure of what to make of this unexpected visitor. A few of the elders muttered to one another, and some of the younger children giggled nervously. Lena, however, could hardly contain her excitement. A storyteller! And not just any storyteller—a traveler who had seen the world and collected stories from distant lands! This was exactly what she had been longing for.

The storyteller smiled at the murmurs in the crowd. "I can see that you are a village that loves stories," he said. "I've heard about your hero, Torin. But the world is wide, my friends, and there are many stories to be told. Stories from lands you have never seen, with heroes who look different from Torin. Would you like to hear one?"

For a moment, the village was silent. The elders, who had always valued the tradition of telling Torin's story, looked uncertain. But then a voice spoke up.

"Yes!" Lena cried out, her voice clear and strong. "I want to hear one!"

The storyteller's eyes twinkled as he turned toward her. "Ah," he said, "I see there is a young one here with a heart open to new stories. Very well, let me tell you a tale from a faraway land—a tale of a girl who lived in the desert, where the sand stretches as far as the eye can see."

The villagers gathered closer, intrigued by this strange new story. Lena's heart beat fast as she sat cross-legged in front of the storyteller, her eyes wide with anticipation.

And so, the storyteller began.

He told of Nia, a young girl who lived in a village on the edge of the desert. Nia's village depended on a hidden oasis for their water, but one year, the oasis dried up. Nia, brave and determined, set out on a dangerous journey across the endless dunes to find a new source of water. Along the way, she encountered creatures of the desert—some friendly, some fierce—and learned valuable lessons about perseverance and the importance of every drop of water.

As the story unfolded, Lena was captivated. Nia's world was so different from hers, yet the girl's bravery reminded her of Torin. But Nia was not like Torin—she was a girl, for one, and she lived in a place that was nothing like their green valley. Still, her courage and determination were universal.

When the story ended, there was a brief moment of silence in the village square. Then, one by one, the villagers began to clap. It was a hesitant applause at first, but it grew louder as they shared glances with one another, impressed by the richness of the tale they had just heard.

Lena's heart soared. This was just the beginning, she knew it. There were so many more stories out there, and she wanted to hear them all.

Lessons Learned

1. Curiosity drives discovery – Lena's desire to hear more stories fuels her desire for knowledge.
2. Tradition brings comfort but can also limit growth – The village's attachment to a single story represents the comfort of tradition but also shows the limitations of hearing only one perspective.
3. Bravery takes many forms – Heroes can look and act differently, but bravery is a universal trait.

4. There is beauty in difference – Lena learns that heroes and stories come from all kinds of places, and every one of them has value.
5. Change can be difficult – The village elders' initial resistance to new stories shows that change can be uncomfortable at first.
6. Everyone has a story worth telling – The storyteller's tales emphasize that every culture and person has valuable stories to share.
7. Imagination opens doors to new worlds – Lena's dreams of hearing new stories reveal the power of imagination.
8. Diverse stories teach new lessons – Through Nia's tale, Lena learns about perseverance and the importance of water, lessons tied to a different culture and environment.
9. Inclusivity means embracing all voices – The villagers' willingness to listen to new stories shows the importance of being open to different perspectives.
10. Storytelling connects people – The storyteller's visit unites the village, showing that stories from faraway places can create bonds across cultures.

Chapter 2: The Arrival of the Storyteller

The night after the storyteller's first visit was filled with a buzz of excitement and quiet conversations that echoed through the narrow streets of Eldena. Though the villagers were used to the rhythms of their life, something had shifted. Lena lay awake in her small bed, staring up at the wooden beams of the ceiling. Her mind raced with the images of Nia from the desert, the creatures she had met, and the struggles she had faced. It was so different from anything Lena had ever imagined, yet it felt real, as if she had traveled with Nia across those scorching sands.

The next morning, Lena rushed to the village square, hoping to catch another glimpse of the storyteller. She wasn't the only one. Other villagers had gathered as well, some curious, others hesitant, but there was a palpable sense that something new had arrived, and it wasn't going to leave easily.

The storyteller stood by his horse, adjusting the saddle and humming a tune. His colorful cloak fluttered in the morning breeze, and the wide-brimmed hat shielded his eyes from the bright sun. As he worked, a small crowd began to form, and Lena pushed her way to the front, eager to hear more.

"Good morning!" the storyteller greeted them with a smile. "It seems my stories have stirred your curiosity."

There were murmurs of agreement from the villagers, though some looked away, unsure of how to respond.

"I travel far and wide," the storyteller continued, "gathering tales from every corner of the world. Each one is unique, but they all share something in common—lessons to be learned, wisdom to be gained."

Lena couldn't contain her excitement any longer. "Will you tell us another one today?"

The storyteller chuckled softly. "Of course, young one. But tell me, what did you learn from Nia's story?"

Lena thought for a moment before answering. "I learned that even if you're small or scared, you can still be brave and do important things."

The storyteller nodded approvingly. "A fine lesson indeed. Stories have the power to teach us about ourselves and the world, no matter where we come from."

The villagers, intrigued by Lena's boldness, began to settle in, eager for the next story. Some still whispered among themselves, questioning whether they should spend more time listening to tales from far-off lands, but others, especially the children, were captivated.

The storyteller raised his hands, signaling the start of a new story. His voice became soft, almost hypnotic, as he began weaving his tale.

"Once, in a land far to the north, where the winds blow cold and the rivers run fast, there lived a boy named Arin. Arin was born with a gift—a golden voice that could calm the fiercest storm and heal the deepest wounds. But Arin was also born blind. From the day he was born, he had never seen the world around him, yet his voice could paint pictures more vivid than any sight."

As the storyteller spoke, the villagers leaned in, their attention focused entirely on the boy named Arin. Lena felt herself being drawn into the story, imagining the icy rivers and the snowy mountains of Arin's world.

"Despite his blindness, Arin was never afraid," the storyteller continued. "He had learned to rely on his other senses—the sound of the wind, the feel of the ground beneath his feet, the scent of the pine trees that surrounded his village. But more than anything, it was his voice that set him apart. When he sang, the birds would gather, the wolves would listen, and even the trees seemed to sway to his melody."

Lena could almost hear the song in her mind, a melody so beautiful that it made her heart ache. Arin's blindness didn't seem like a limitation; instead, it made him special, someone whose gift could touch the world in ways others couldn't.

"One winter," the storyteller continued, his voice dropping to a hushed tone, "a terrible illness swept through Arin's village. Many fell ill, including Arin's own mother. The villagers were desperate. They had no healer, no medicine to cure the sickness that had come with the cold winds. But Arin, though he could not see, felt the pain in the voices of those around him. He knew that something had to be done."

The tension in the square grew as the storyteller paused, letting the weight of the moment sink in. Lena's heart raced, wondering what Arin would do.

"Arin decided to use his voice, his one true gift, to try and save his mother and the other villagers. He stood in the center of the village and began to sing. His voice soared over the rooftops, echoing through the valley, and soon, the wind itself seemed to calm. The people, weak and weary, stopped in their tracks, drawn to the sound. As Arin sang, something magical began to happen. The illness that had gripped the village slowly began to lift. Those who had been on the brink of death found new strength. The air felt warmer, and the sickness retreated."

The storyteller's words hung in the air like a spell. Lena could feel the emotions of the villagers in the story—relief, hope, and awe at Arin's power.

"Arin's voice," the storyteller said softly, "was a gift unlike any other. He could not see the world, but his voice allowed him to touch it in ways that no one else could. And from that day forward, the people of his village honored Arin not for what he couldn't do, but for what he could. His blindness did not make him weak; it made him strong in ways they had never imagined."

As the storyteller finished, there was a moment of silence in the square. The villagers seemed to be holding their breath, absorbing the story they had just heard. Lena's mind was racing. Arin's story had touched her deeply, not just because of his bravery but because of the way he used his gift to help others. His blindness wasn't a limitation—it was simply a part of who he was, and it didn't stop him from making a difference.

The storyteller smiled gently at the crowd. "What do you think, my friends? What did you learn from Arin's story?"

This time, it wasn't just Lena who answered. A boy from the back of the crowd spoke up. "I learned that everyone has something special about them, even if it's not something you can see."

Another villager, an older woman, nodded thoughtfully. "I never thought about it that way before. We all have different gifts, don't we?"

The storyteller nodded. "Indeed. We all have gifts, and sometimes the most powerful ones are those that are not immediately visible. Arin's voice was his way of seeing the world, and through it, he touched the hearts of many."

Lena's mother, who had been watching from the edge of the crowd, stepped forward. "It's true," she said quietly. "We've spent so long telling only one story. Maybe it's time we started listening to others."

The storyteller smiled warmly. "That is the beauty of stories. They show us what we might not see on our own. They open our hearts to new possibilities."

The villagers murmured in agreement, and Lena felt a surge of hope. Maybe, just maybe, her village was ready to change. Maybe they could learn from the stories of others, just as she had.

As the crowd began to disperse, the storyteller looked down at Lena, his eyes twinkling. "You have a gift too, young one," he said. "A gift for seeing the value in stories. Never lose that."

Lena beamed. She had never felt more alive, more certain that she was on the path to something wonderful.

Lessons Learned

1. Everyone has a unique gift, even if it isn't immediately visible.
2. Limitations can become strengths if we find ways to embrace them.

3. People often judge based on what they see, but true power lies beyond appearances.
4. Stories from different places can teach us new ways of thinking about ourselves and others.
5. Gifts aren't always physical; sometimes they are emotional or spiritual.
6. The way we perceive people can change when we learn their story.
7. Communities can benefit from the talents of all their members, even those with perceived differences.
8. Listening to others' stories can open our hearts to new possibilities.
9. There is power in empathy and understanding different perspectives.
10. Being different doesn't make someone less valuable; it often makes them more special.

Chapter 3: A Tale of the Desert

The next morning, the village square was filled with a sense of eager anticipation. News of the storyteller's captivating tales had spread, and more villagers had gathered, waiting to hear what new wonders he might share. Even some of the elders, who had been skeptical at first, were now intrigued by the idea of hearing stories from far-off lands. Lena stood at the front, her heart pounding with excitement. She could hardly wait to hear what story the storyteller would share today.

As the villagers settled in, the storyteller greeted them with a warm smile. His horse stood beside him, its saddle packed with bags full of treasures from distant places—scrolls, books, and trinkets that hinted at the vastness of the world beyond Eldena.

"Good morning, my friends," the storyteller said, his voice rich and melodious. "It seems you are all ready for another journey today."

The villagers murmured in agreement, and the storyteller nodded. "Very well, then. Today, I shall take you to a land where the sun beats down on endless stretches of golden sand. It is a land of harsh beauty, where life clings to the edges of survival. But it is also a land of courage, where even the smallest creature has a role to play. Let me tell you the story of a girl named Nia, who lived on the edge of the desert and embarked on a journey that would change her life forever."

The crowd fell silent as the storyteller began his tale. Lena, perched at the edge of her seat, could feel the heat of the desert in her mind, imagining the vast, sandy dunes stretching as far as the eye could see.

"Nia was no older than you, Lena," the storyteller said, his eyes glinting as he looked at her. "She lived in a village that depended on a hidden oasis for water. But one year, the oasis began to dry up, and the people of her village grew desperate. Without the water from the oasis, they could not survive the brutal heat of the desert. The elders gathered and discussed what to do, but no one had a solution. The desert was vast, and the location of any other oasis was unknown."

Lena leaned forward, her breath catching in her throat. She could imagine the desperation of Nia's village, the fear that must have gripped them as their precious water began to disappear.

"But Nia," the storyteller continued, "was not one to sit and wait for a solution to come to her. She had always been a curious girl, much like you, Lena. She believed that if she set out into the desert, she could find a new oasis and save her village. The elders were doubtful. They said that no one had ever survived a journey into the deep desert, especially not someone as young as Nia. But Nia was determined. She knew that her small size didn't mean she was weak, and her age didn't mean she couldn't be brave."

The villagers listened intently, drawn into the tale. Even the children, who often grew restless during long stories, were quiet, captivated by the image of Nia standing at the edge of the desert, ready to face the unknown.

"With nothing but a small bag of supplies and her faith in herself, Nia set out into the desert. The sun beat down on her, and the sand shifted beneath her feet, making every step a challenge. But Nia didn't give up. She knew that somewhere out there, beyond the horizon, there had to be water."

As the storyteller described Nia's journey, Lena felt the weight of the heat and the endless sand. She could see Nia, trudging through the dunes, her determination unwavering despite the odds stacked against her.

"The desert was full of dangers," the storyteller said, his voice dropping to a whisper. "There were creatures hidden in the sand, waiting for a careless step. There were whirlwinds that could blind a traveler in seconds, and the nights were as cold as the days were hot. But Nia faced each challenge with courage. She listened to the sounds of the desert—the whisper of the wind, the scurrying of the small creatures beneath the sand—and she learned to navigate her way by the stars, just as her ancestors had done long ago."

Lena's heart raced as she imagined Nia facing these dangers. The desert was so different from her own village, but the lessons Nia was learning felt universal—bravery, perseverance, and the importance of listening to the world around you.

"After days of walking, when Nia thought she could go no further, she saw something in the distance. It was a glimmer of green—tiny at first, but it grew larger as she got closer. With the last of her strength, she climbed the final dune, and there, nestled in a small valley, she found it—a new oasis, hidden from the rest of the world."

The villagers gasped, their eyes wide with wonder. Lena could feel the relief that must have washed over Nia as she gazed upon the life-giving water.

"But Nia's journey wasn't over yet," the storyteller said, his voice growing serious. "She still had to find her way back to her village. And as she turned to leave the oasis, she realized something important. The journey had changed her. She was no longer the same girl who had left the village days before. She had faced the desert, the unknown, and had come out stronger. She knew that no matter what challenges she faced in the future, she would always find a way to overcome them."

As the storyteller finished, the square was silent once more. Lena could feel the weight of Nia's journey, the strength it had taken to face the unknown and to trust in herself when no one else believed in her. It was a story that spoke not just to the challenges of survival, but to the power of believing in one's own abilities, even when the world seemed impossible to conquer.

Lessons Learned

1. Bravery comes in all forms, regardless of size or age.
2. Perseverance is key to overcoming even the greatest challenges.

3. Facing the unknown can lead to personal growth and transformation.
4. Listening to the world around you can help guide you through difficult times.
5. Every journey teaches us something about ourselves.
6. Trusting in yourself is often the first step toward success.
7. The greatest challenges are sometimes the ones we face within ourselves.
8. Believing in your own strength can inspire others to do the same.
9. New experiences can change who we are and make us stronger.
10. Courage is not the absence of fear, but the determination to move forward despite it.

Chapter 4: The Boy with the Golden Voice

The village of Eldena had begun to change, slowly but surely. The stories shared by the mysterious storyteller had ignited something within the people—an awareness that the world was far larger and more diverse than they had ever imagined. Though some villagers still clung to the familiarity of Torin's tale, others, especially the children, were eager for more. Lena, with her ever-growing curiosity, found herself thinking constantly about the characters she had met through the stories—the brave Nia from the desert, and now, a new hero was about to enter her life.

One morning, as the villagers gathered once again in the square, there was a palpable sense of anticipation. The sun was still rising over the mountains, casting a warm golden light over the village, and the storyteller, with his colorful cloak and wide-brimmed hat, stood in the center of the square, waiting for the crowd to settle.

Lena found her usual spot at the front, her eyes fixed on the storyteller, wondering what new adventure would unfold today. She had heard stories of deserts and oases, of faraway lands where the landscape itself was a challenge to overcome. But today, the storyteller had something different in mind.

"Today," the storyteller began, his voice calm and steady, "I will tell you the story of a boy named Kian, who lived in a village much like yours. But Kian was different. He was born without the ability to see."

A murmur ran through the crowd. Blindness was something that many of the villagers didn't understand. How could someone who couldn't see live in the world, much less do something heroic?

"But," the storyteller continued, "Kian had a gift. He possessed a golden voice, a voice so beautiful and powerful that it could calm storms, heal wounds, and bring peace to those in need. His voice was his way of seeing the world, and through it, he touched the lives of many."

As the storyteller spoke, Lena's mind filled with images of Kian, a boy who couldn't see the world around him but could feel it deeply through the power of his voice. She imagined him walking through his village, his eyes closed, but his ears and heart wide open.

"Kian's village," the storyteller said, "was nestled deep in the mountains, surrounded by forests and rivers. The people there lived simple lives, farming the land and raising their families. But one year, a terrible storm struck the village. The rivers overflowed, and the crops were washed away. The people were frightened, for they had never seen such devastation before. The storm seemed never-ending, and soon, hope began to fade."

The villagers of Eldena listened intently, their faces reflecting the growing tension in the story. They could imagine the fear that must have gripped Kian's village, the sense of helplessness as the storm raged on, relentless and unforgiving.

"But Kian," the storyteller continued, "though he could not see the storm, could feel it in the air. He could hear the wind howling through the trees, the water rushing down the mountainside. And he knew that his village needed something more than just strength to survive—they needed hope. And so, Kian did what he did best. He sang."

Lena's heart leaped. She could almost hear Kian's voice in her mind, a melody so pure and powerful that it could reach the heavens themselves. She imagined the villagers, standing in the pouring rain, listening to the sound of Kian's song rising above the storm.

"As Kian's voice filled the air," the storyteller said, his own voice growing softer, "something miraculous happened. The storm, which had raged for days, began to calm. The winds softened, the rain slowed, and the dark clouds began to part. It was as if Kian's song had touched the storm itself, bringing peace where there had only been chaos."

The villagers of Eldena were silent, enraptured by the magic of the story. Even those who had been skeptical of the storyteller's tales were moved by the image of Kian standing in the rain, his golden voice cutting through the darkness.

"But Kian's song," the storyteller said, "was not just for the storm. It was for the people of his village, who had lost hope. Through his voice, he reminded them that they were not alone, that they had the strength to rebuild, to start again. And that is exactly what they did. With Kian's song in their hearts, the villagers set to work, clearing the debris, replanting the crops, and rebuilding their homes."

The storyteller paused, allowing the weight of the story to settle over the crowd. Lena felt a lump in her throat. Kian's story was so different from anything she had heard before. It wasn't about fighting with swords or battling monsters. It was about using the gifts you have, even when they're not the ones people expect.

"Kian," the storyteller said, "remained in his village for the rest of his life, his voice a constant source of comfort and strength for those around him. He could not see the world, but through his song, he helped others see the beauty in life, even in the darkest times."

As the story ended, the villagers sat in silence for a moment, absorbing the lessons Kian's story had to offer. Then, slowly, they began to clap. It wasn't the enthusiastic applause that had followed Nia's tale, but a quieter, more thoughtful recognition of the power of the story they had just heard.

Lena, her mind still filled with the sound of Kian's song, turned to look at the villagers around her. She could see that Kian's story had touched them deeply. Some of the older villagers, who had been hesitant to embrace the new stories, seemed moved by the idea that someone like Kian—someone who couldn't see—could still make such a profound impact.

The storyteller smiled gently at the crowd. "Kian's story," he said, "reminds us that our strengths are not always the ones people expect. Sometimes, the greatest gifts come from within, and they are the ones that can change the world."

Lena felt a warmth in her chest as she listened to the storyteller's words. She had always believed that everyone had something special to offer, but Kian's story had made that belief even stronger. It didn't matter if you were small, or if you couldn't see, or if you were different from those around you—what mattered was how you used the gifts you had been given.

Lessons Learned

1. Strength comes in many forms, not just physical abilities.
2. Our gifts are not always visible, but they can still make a difference.
3. Hope can come from unexpected places, even in the darkest times.
4. Everyone has something valuable to contribute, regardless of their limitations.
5. True power lies in using your unique talents to help others.
6. You don't have to be like everyone else to make an impact.
7. Music and art have the power to heal and bring people together.
8. Sometimes, the most important battles are the ones fought with kindness and compassion.
9. The greatest heroes are often the ones who use their gifts to lift others up.
10. Believing in yourself and your abilities can inspire others to do the same.

Chapter 5: The Story of the Moon and Stars

The following morning, the village of Eldena was alive with whispers of the storyteller's latest tale. Kian's story had moved the villagers deeply, and even those who had once resisted the idea of hearing new stories were beginning to soften. Lena could feel the change in the air—it was as if the village itself was opening up, ready to embrace the world beyond its borders.

Lena, as always, was one of the first to arrive in the square, eager to hear the next story. She had spent much of the previous night thinking about Kian and his golden voice, wondering what it would be like to have a gift so powerful that it could change the world around you. But today, as the storyteller prepared to share another tale, Lena sensed that this story would take her in a different direction, one that reached far beyond the earth and into the sky.

The storyteller stood before the gathered villagers, his eyes twinkling with the light of the early morning sun. His colorful cloak fluttered in the breeze, and his wide-brimmed hat cast a shadow over his face, giving him an air of mystery. As the villagers settled in, he began to speak.

"Today," the storyteller said, his voice low and reverent, "I will tell you a story from a land far to the east, where the people believe that the moon and stars are the guiding lights of the world. It is a story of faith, of wonder, and of the power of the night sky. Let me take you to a village where the people live by the light of the stars, and where a young girl named Aislin learned to read the sky like a map."

Lena's eyes widened with excitement. She had always been fascinated by the stars, by the way they twinkled and shimmered in the darkness. The idea that someone could read the stars, like words on a page, filled her with awe.

"In Aislin's village," the storyteller continued, "the night sky was everything. The people believed that the stars were the eyes of their ancestors, watching over them, guiding them through the challenges of life. They believed that the moon was a great protector, lighting the way in the darkness and keeping them safe from harm."

The villagers of Eldena listened closely, their faces reflecting the wonder of the world the storyteller was painting for them. Aislin's village was so different from their own—rooted in a deep connection to the stars and the moon, with faith that the sky above them held the answers to life's mysteries.

"Aislin," the storyteller said, "was a quiet, thoughtful girl, always gazing up at the sky, wondering what secrets the stars held. She had heard the stories of her ancestors, how they had used the stars to navigate the seas and the forests, how they had read the night sky like a map that led them to safety. But Aislin wanted to do more than just wonder—she wanted to learn how to read the stars herself."

Lena felt a connection to Aislin, to her quiet curiosity and her desire to understand the world around her. She knew what it was like to feel a yearning for knowledge, to want to explore the unknown.

"Aislin's village was preparing for a great journey," the storyteller said, his voice growing more intense. "Every year, they traveled to the sacred mountain, a place where they believed the stars touched the earth, where they could feel the presence of their ancestors more clearly than anywhere else. But this year, there was a problem. The night before they were set to leave, a great fog rolled in, covering the sky in a thick, impenetrable mist. The stars, their guiding lights, were hidden from view."

The villagers of Eldena gasped softly. They could imagine the panic that must have spread through Aislin's village, the fear of being lost without the stars to guide them.

"The elders of the village were at a loss," the storyteller continued. "Without the stars, they could not make the journey. They could not find the sacred mountain without the map that the night sky provided. But Aislin, though young and inexperienced, felt a deep certainty in her heart. She believed that the stars were still there, hidden behind the fog, and that if she listened closely, she could still find her way."

Lena's heart pounded in her chest. Aislin's faith in the stars, even when they couldn't be seen, reminded her of the lessons she had learned from Kian's story—the idea that sometimes, the most important things aren't visible, but they are always there, guiding us.

"With nothing but her trust in the night sky," the storyteller said, his voice rising with excitement, "Aislin stepped forward. She closed her eyes and listened to the wind, felt the cool air on her skin, and let the rhythm of the earth guide her. Slowly, she began to walk, leading her village through the fog, trusting that the stars would reveal themselves when the time was right."

Lena held her breath, imagining Aislin walking through the mist, her village following behind her, all eyes on the sky.

"As they walked," the storyteller continued, "the fog began to lift, ever so slowly. And just as Aislin had believed, the stars began to emerge from behind the clouds, one by one, until the sky was once again filled with their guiding light. Aislin had led her village to safety, not by sight, but by faith in the stars and in her own intuition."

The villagers of Eldena exhaled as one, their tension melting away as the story reached its climax. Lena felt a surge of pride for Aislin, for her bravery and her quiet confidence. She had trusted in something greater than herself, something that couldn't be seen but could always be felt.

"Aislin's journey," the storyteller said, his voice softening once more, "reminded her village of the power of the stars and the moon, of the importance of faith, even when the way forward seems unclear. And from that day on, Aislin was known as the girl who could read the stars, a guide for her people through the darkest of nights."

As the storyteller finished, the square was filled with a quiet reverence. The villagers seemed to be lost in thought, contemplating

the deeper meaning of Aislin's story. Even Lena, who had always been curious about the world beyond her village, felt a new sense of wonder about the night sky, about the stars that watched over them all.

The storyteller smiled at the crowd. "The stars and the moon are always with us," he said. "They remind us that even when we can't see the way forward, there is always something guiding us, if we are willing to listen."

Lena couldn't stop thinking about Aislin as she walked home that evening. The idea that the stars could be more than just points of light in the sky, that they could hold wisdom and guidance, filled her with awe. She wondered if she, too, could learn to read the stars, to trust in something beyond what she could see.

Lessons Learned

1. Faith can guide us through uncertain times, even when the path isn't clear.
2. Trusting in something greater than ourselves can lead us to safety and understanding.
3. The stars and the moon have been symbols of guidance and protection for many cultures.
4. Even when we can't see what lies ahead, there is always something guiding us.
5. Listening to the world around us can reveal hidden truths and lead us to new discoveries.
6. Patience and belief in ourselves can help us overcome seemingly insurmountable challenges.
7. Sometimes the answers we seek are hidden, waiting for the right moment to be revealed.
8. Quiet confidence and trust in our intuition can lead to great achievements.
9. The night sky holds ancient wisdom, waiting to be unlocked by those willing to listen.

10. There is power in believing in things we cannot see but can feel deeply within us.

Chapter 6: The Fear of the Unknown

As the storyteller's tales continued to spread through the village of Eldena, excitement and curiosity grew among many of the younger villagers, but not everyone shared their enthusiasm. The elders, who had lived their entire lives within the safety of the village, began to express their concerns more openly. While some stories brought new wisdom and joy, others stirred fear and uncertainty.

Lena had noticed this growing tension. The joy she had felt after each story, the thrill of hearing about distant lands and brave characters, seemed to be lost on some of the older villagers. Her parents, usually supportive and kind, had begun to worry about her eagerness to hear more stories. They weren't alone in their concerns. Each night, after the villagers dispersed from the square, Lena overheard whispers—quiet, fearful conversations that hinted at an unease creeping into the minds of the adults.

One evening, as Lena sat by the fire with her parents, the atmosphere in their small home felt different. Her mother was stirring a pot of soup, but her movements were slower than usual. Her father, who often hummed as he whittled pieces of wood, was silent. Lena, sensing the weight of their thoughts, finally spoke up.

"Is something wrong?" she asked, looking between her parents.

Her father glanced at her mother before setting down the small wooden figure he had been carving. "Lena, we've been meaning to talk to you," he said, his voice gentle but serious. "These stories you've been so eager to hear... They're not like the stories we grew up with. They're strange, from places we don't know. People are starting to wonder if maybe they're dangerous."

"Dangerous?" Lena repeated, her eyes widening. "How could a story be dangerous?"

Her mother sighed, turning to face her. "It's not the stories themselves, Lena. It's what they're doing to the village. People are starting to change, to think differently. And when things change too quickly, it can be scary. Some of the elders are worried that these stories are making us forget who we are, forget our traditions."

Lena felt a pang of confusion and frustration. She had never imagined that hearing new stories could be seen as something harmful. "But the stories are teaching us new things," she argued. "They're showing us that there's more to the world than just this village. Isn't that a good thing?"

Her father shook his head, though his expression remained soft. "It's not that simple, Lena. This village has survived for generations because we've held onto what we know. Torin's story is part of who we are. It reminds us of our strength, our unity. These new stories, while they may be interesting, they don't belong here. They might make people question things, make them want to leave, or worse... forget where they come from."

Lena was silent for a moment, processing her father's words. She understood that the village cherished its traditions, that the story of Torin had been a foundation for their community for as long as anyone could remember. But she couldn't help but feel that the new stories didn't take away from that—they added to it, enriching their understanding of the world.

"But what if we can have both?" Lena asked quietly. "What if we can still honor Torin's story and also learn from these new ones?"

Her mother knelt beside her, placing a hand on Lena's shoulder. "We don't want you to stop learning, Lena. But we need you to understand that not everyone is ready for these changes. The world outside is full of things we don't know, and that can be frightening for some people."

Lena nodded, though her heart still ached with the desire to hear more stories, to learn more about the world beyond the mountains. She couldn't shake the feeling that the fear gripping the village wasn't about the stories themselves, but about the unknown—the idea that there was more out there than they had ever imagined, and that scared them.

The next day, as the storyteller arrived in the square, Lena noticed that the crowd was smaller than usual. Some of the elders were absent, and a few of the adults lingered at the edges of the square, watching but not joining the circle that had formed around the storyteller.

The storyteller, however, seemed unfazed by the smaller audience. He greeted those who had come with the same warmth and enthusiasm as always, his eyes twinkling as he prepared to share another tale. But Lena could see the tension in the air, could feel the unease settling over the village like a cloud.

"Today," the storyteller began, his voice steady and calming, "I will tell you a story about fear—about the fear of the unknown, and how it can shape our lives if we let it."

Lena's heart quickened. It was as if the storyteller had sensed the growing unease in the village, the fear that was quietly spreading among the adults. She leaned forward, eager to hear what wisdom this new story would bring.

"Long ago, in a village much like this one," the storyteller said, "there lived a people who knew only one way of life. They had never traveled beyond the mountains that surrounded them, never ventured into the forests or across the rivers. They were content with what they knew, and for many generations, they lived peacefully."

The villagers listened in silence, some nodding as if the story echoed their own lives.

"But one day," the storyteller continued, "a young woman named Mara began to wonder about the world beyond the mountains. She had always felt a pull toward the unknown, a curiosity about what lay on the other side. But every time she spoke of her desire to explore, the elders of the village warned her against it. 'The world outside is dangerous,' they told her. 'We don't know what's out there, and it's better to stay where we're safe.'"

Lena could feel the tension in the story building. Mara's curiosity reminded her of her own, her desire to learn more about the world beyond Eldena.

"But Mara couldn't ignore the pull in her heart," the storyteller said. "One night, while the village slept, she packed a small bag and set out on a journey beyond the mountains. At first, the world beyond seemed strange and overwhelming. The trees were taller, the rivers wider, and the creatures she encountered were unlike anything she had ever seen. But Mara was not afraid. She embraced the unknown, trusting in her ability to navigate whatever came her way."

The villagers shifted uneasily. Some of the younger ones were enraptured by the story, while a few of the older ones exchanged wary glances.

"As Mara traveled," the storyteller continued, "she discovered wonders she had never imagined. She met people who spoke different languages, who lived in ways that were completely unfamiliar to her. But instead of fear, Mara felt a deep sense of connection. She realized that though the world outside was different, it was also full of beauty and wisdom."

Lena smiled, feeling a surge of hope. Mara's journey was a reflection of what she had always believed—that the unknown wasn't something to be feared, but something to be embraced.

"But when Mara returned to her village," the storyteller said, his voice growing more somber, "she found that not everyone was ready to hear about her journey. The elders, who had always warned against venturing beyond the mountains, refused to listen to her stories. They were afraid that if the village heard about the world outside, they would begin to question their way of life, to doubt the traditions that had kept them safe for so long."

Lena felt a knot form in her stomach. She could see the parallels between Mara's village and her own. The fear that gripped Mara's elders was the same fear she saw in the eyes of some of the adults in Eldena.

Chapter 7: The Story of a Brave, Silent Girl

The tension in the village hadn't completely disappeared, but it had shifted. The villagers who had been most vocal about their fears had grown quieter, though they still watched with wary eyes as the storyteller continued to weave his tales. But despite the uncertainty, more and more people were coming to listen, drawn by the magic of the stories and the lessons they brought. Lena, always at the front of the crowd, felt a growing sense of responsibility. The storyteller's tales were opening minds, and she wanted to be part of the change, to help her village see the value in every story.

One morning, as the sun began to rise over the mountains, the storyteller arrived in the square with a somber look on his face. His cloak, though still vibrant, seemed to sway a little more slowly in the breeze, and there was a quietness in his movements that made Lena wonder what kind of story he would share that day. The crowd gathered as usual, but there was a hush in the air, as if everyone sensed that something different was coming.

"Today," the storyteller began, his voice soft but clear, "I will tell you the story of a girl who spoke not with words, but with her heart. It is a story of bravery, of strength, and of the power that comes from truly listening."

Lena's curiosity piqued immediately. She had heard many stories about heroes who spoke with boldness, who rallied people with their words. But a girl who didn't speak? How could she show bravery without a voice?

"In a village far from here," the storyteller continued, "there lived a girl named Liora. From the day she was born, Liora had never spoken a single word. The people of her village didn't know why, and many assumed she simply couldn't. They believed that without words, she could not lead, could not make a difference. And so, Liora was often overlooked, her silence mistaken for weakness."

Lena's heart ached for Liora. She could imagine what it must have been like to be ignored, to have others assume that just because you didn't speak, you had nothing to offer. It was a feeling she had experienced in small ways when the adults in her village dismissed her questions, but for Liora, it seemed much worse.

"But Liora was not weak," the storyteller said, his voice growing stronger. "Though she could not speak, she had a mind as sharp as any, and a heart full of compassion. She observed the world around her, noticing things that others missed. She saw the way the wind moved through the trees, the way the animals communicated without words. And most of all, she listened—listened to the sounds of her village, to the stories that were told, and to the emotions that people carried in their voices, even when they didn't say a word."

Lena felt a deep admiration for Liora. The girl's ability to listen so intently, to understand the world through observation and empathy, was something Lena had never thought about before. She had always believed that words were the most important way to communicate, but Liora's story was showing her something different.

"One day," the storyteller continued, "a great conflict arose in Liora's village. A neighboring village had begun to encroach on their land, and tensions were rising. The leaders of the two villages met to discuss a solution, but the talks quickly turned into arguments. Voices were raised, tempers flared, and it seemed that war was inevitable."

The villagers of Eldena leaned in, their expressions tense. They knew all too well the dangers of conflict, the way fear and anger could tear communities apart.

"Liora watched from the edges of the meeting, her eyes taking in every detail, her ears attuned to the voices around her. She could hear the anger, the frustration, but she also heard something else—something that no one else seemed to notice. Beneath the harsh words and raised voices, there was fear. Both villages were afraid—afraid of losing their homes, their way of life. And in that fear, they had forgotten how to listen to one another."

Lena's heart pounded. She could feel the weight of the moment, the tension that must have filled the air as the two villages stood on the brink of war. But what could Liora do? How could she make a difference if no one would listen to her?

"Without a word," the storyteller said, "Liora stepped into the middle of the gathering. The leaders, startled by her presence, fell silent. They had always known her as the quiet girl, the one who never spoke, and they were curious to see what she would do."

The crowd in Eldena was silent, hanging on every word. Lena could feel the anticipation building inside her, wondering what Liora's next move would be.

"Liora stood before them," the storyteller continued, "and without speaking, she began to mimic their gestures, their raised hands, their clenched fists. She showed them what they looked like in their anger, holding up a mirror to their behavior. And then, with a single gesture, she placed her hand over her heart." Lena's breath caught in her throat. Liora wasn't speaking, but her actions were saying more than words ever could.

"The leaders watched in silence," the storyteller said, "as Liora moved her hand from her heart to her ear, signaling them to listen—to truly listen to one another. Slowly, the anger in the room began to dissipate. The leaders, humbled by her silent wisdom, realized that they had been speaking without hearing, arguing without understanding. And so, they sat down, and for the first time, they began to listen."

The villagers of Eldena were transfixed, their eyes wide with awe. Lena felt a surge of emotion, her heart swelling with admiration for Liora's quiet bravery. She had done what no one else could—she had brought peace without uttering a single word.

Lessons Learned

1. Strength can be found in silence and observation.
2. Listening is just as important as speaking.
3. Empathy can bridge divides and bring peace in times of conflict.
4. Communication isn't just about words—actions can speak volumes.
5. True leadership comes from understanding, not just commanding.
6. Sometimes, the quietest people have the most to teach us.
7. Conflicts can often be resolved by truly hearing each other's fears and concerns.
8. Wisdom can be expressed in ways beyond language.
9. Bravery isn't always loud; it can be found in quiet determination.
10. We should never underestimate the power of listening with our hearts, not just our ears.

Chapter 8: A Story of Many Colors

The village of Eldena had seen many changes since the storyteller first arrived. New stories had woven their way into the hearts of the villagers, changing how they viewed the world and themselves. Though some still clung to the old ways, there was an undeniable shift in the air—a growing curiosity and a hunger for more. The stories had stirred something deep within the people, especially within the children, who eagerly gathered in the square every time the storyteller returned.

One bright morning, the villagers gathered once again, their faces turned toward the storyteller with anticipation. Even those who had been hesitant to listen in the beginning now found themselves drawn to the tales, unable to resist the magic they brought. Lena, as always, was at the front of the crowd, her eyes wide with excitement. She could feel that today's story would be different, special somehow.

The storyteller stood before them, his colorful cloak catching the sunlight, its vibrant patterns almost dancing in the breeze. He smiled at the crowd, his eyes twinkling with warmth. "Today," he began, his voice rich and inviting, "I will tell you a story of a land where the people come in every color imaginable, and each one brings something unique and beautiful to their world."

The villagers leaned in, intrigued. A land of many colors? Lena's mind raced with possibilities. She had seen different shades of skin in the few travelers who had passed through Eldena over the years, but a place where everyone was different? It sounded like a dream, a world where color itself was celebrated.

"In this land," the storyteller continued, "the people lived in harmony, for they understood that their differences were what made them strong. They had learned long ago that every color, every shade, was a gift, something to be cherished and valued. And so, they built a village where each home was painted in the colors of its inhabitants, a rainbow of houses that shimmered in the sunlight."

Lena could almost see the village in her mind—bright, colorful houses lining the streets, each one unique, just like the people who lived within them. It was a beautiful image, one that made her heart swell with joy.

"But it wasn't always this way," the storyteller said, his voice growing more serious. "There was a time when the people of this land did not understand the beauty of their differences. They were afraid of those who didn't look like them, and so, they kept to themselves, building walls around their homes and their hearts."

The crowd was silent, listening intently. Lena felt a pang of sadness. She could imagine the fear that must have gripped the people in the beginning, the way they must have turned away from one another, not realizing the richness they were missing.

"One day," the storyteller continued, "a child was born who was unlike any other. Her skin was the color of the evening sky, deep and rich, with a hint of starlight shimmering just beneath the surface. Her hair flowed like silver, catching the light in ways no one had ever seen before. The people were both awed and frightened. They had never seen anyone like her, and they didn't know what to make of her."

Lena held her breath, her heart aching for the child. She could feel the tension in the story, the weight of being different in a world that didn't yet understand the beauty of diversity.

"As the child grew," the storyteller said, "she noticed that the people around her kept their distance. They whispered about her, unsure of what to think. She was different, and in their eyes, different meant dangerous. But the child, whose name was Zaria, didn't let their fear stop her from exploring the world. She loved the colors of the world—the bright blues of the sky, the rich greens of the trees, and the warm golds of the sun. She longed to share her love of color with the people, to show them that her difference was something to be celebrated, not feared."

The villagers listened quietly, some exchanging glances with one another. Lena could feel the weight of the story pressing down on them all. She knew what it was like to feel different, to have people look at you strangely just because you wanted to explore new ideas. But Zaria's difference was something even more visible, and Lena could only imagine how lonely it must have felt.

"One day," the storyteller continued, "Zaria decided to paint her house. She gathered colors from the earth, from the flowers, and from the sky itself. She mixed them together, creating hues that no one had ever seen before. And then, she began to paint. She covered her home in swirling patterns of blue, silver, gold, and green, the colors blending together in a way that made the house shimmer and glow in the sunlight. It was the most beautiful thing anyone had ever seen."

The villagers gasped softly, their eyes wide with wonder. Lena could picture the house in her mind, its colors dancing in the light, a beacon of beauty and hope.

"But still," the storyteller said, his voice dropping to a whisper, "the people were afraid. They didn't understand how something so different could be so beautiful. And so, they kept their distance, watching from afar but never stepping closer."

Lena's heart ached for Zaria. She had created something so beautiful, something that reflected her unique spirit, and yet the people still couldn't see past their fear.

"Then one evening," the storyteller continued, "a storm rolled in. The winds howled, the rain poured down, and the village was thrown into chaos. Trees were uprooted, houses were damaged, and the people were afraid for their lives. But in the midst of the storm, Zaria's house stood strong, its colors shining even through the darkness. The people, desperate for shelter, made their way to her home, seeking refuge from the storm."

Lena could feel the tension building in the story, her breath catching in her throat. What would happen when the people came to Zaria's door? Would they finally see her for who she was?

"As the people gathered at her door," the storyteller said, "Zaria welcomed them in with open arms. She gave them warmth, food, and comfort, asking for nothing in return. And as they sat together in her brightly colored home, the people began to realize that it wasn't Zaria's difference that had made them afraid—it was their own inability to see the beauty in what they didn't understand."

The villagers of Eldena were silent, the weight of the storyteller's words sinking in. Lena felt a lump rise in her throat. She knew that feeling—the fear of the unknown, the way it could blind people to the truth. But Zaria's story was a reminder that differences were not something to be feared; they were something to be celebrated.

"When the storm finally passed," the storyteller continued, "the people emerged from Zaria's home with new eyes. They saw the colors of the world in a different light, understanding that every shade, every hue, brought something valuable to their lives. From that day on, the people of the village began to paint their own homes in the colors that reflected their spirits, creating a rainbow of houses that shimmered in the sunlight. And Zaria, the girl who had once been feared for her difference, became a symbol of beauty and unity in the village."

Lena felt tears prick at the corners of her eyes, moved by the story of Zaria and her bravery. She had taken something that made her different and turned it into a gift for her community, showing them the power of embracing diversity.

Lessons Learned

1. Our differences are what make the world beautiful and unique.
2. Fear of the unknown often blinds us to the beauty in others.
3. Embracing diversity can strengthen and unite communities.

4. True bravery comes from being yourself, even when others don't understand.
5. Judging others based on appearances prevents us from seeing their true value.
6. Everyone brings something valuable to the world, no matter how different they are.
7. Unity is built on accepting and celebrating differences.
8. Acts of kindness and understanding can change people's hearts.
9. Creativity and self-expression are powerful tools for breaking down barriers.
10. By embracing the colors of the world, we create a brighter, more inclusive future.

Chapter 9: The Power of Friendship

The morning sun bathed the village of Eldena in a soft, golden light, casting long shadows across the square where the villagers gathered once again. There was a palpable sense of anticipation in the air as the storyteller prepared to share yet another tale. By now, the villagers had come to expect that each story would bring something new, a lesson that would resonate with them long after the storyteller had finished speaking. And today, Lena felt a particular excitement bubbling inside her. She had always loved stories about friendships—about the bonds that connected people, no matter how different they were. Somehow, she sensed that today's story would be about just that.

The storyteller stood before them, his cloak swaying gently in the breeze. His face, as always, was filled with warmth and wisdom, and as he looked out at the crowd, he smiled. "Today," he began, his voice strong and clear, "I will tell you a story of two friends, different in every way but bound together by a connection that neither distance nor differences could break."

Lena's heart leaped. She loved stories about friendship, about how people could come together despite their differences and find strength in one another. She leaned forward, eager to hear what would unfold.

"In a land far to the west," the storyteller continued, "there lived two villages, separated by a great river. One village was nestled in the hills, where the people were strong and tall, their skin kissed by the sun, their hands rough from working the land. The other village lay in a valley, where the people were small and nimble, their skin pale from the shade of the trees, their hands quick from weaving and crafting. Though the villages were only a river apart, they had little contact with one another. They spoke different languages, wore different clothes, and lived in different ways. And so, for many years, they remained separate, content in their own worlds."

The villagers of Eldena listened closely, their faces reflecting the growing interest in the story. Lena could feel the tension building, the divide between the two villages mirroring the divisions she had seen in her own village at times.

"But there were two children," the storyteller said, "who were not content to remain apart. One was a boy named Milo, from the village in the hills, and the other was a girl named Leira, from the village in the valley. Though they had never met, they both loved to explore, to wander to the edge of their villages and dream of what lay on the other side of the river. They were both curious, eager to learn about the world beyond their own homes."

Lena smiled to herself. She could already see where the story was going, and it filled her with excitement. Milo and Leira reminded her of herself—the way they longed to explore, to learn about the world beyond the familiar.

"One day," the storyteller continued, "Milo decided to cross the river. He had always wondered what the people in the valley were like, and his curiosity finally got the better of him. He built a small raft and, under the cover of night, set out across the water. On the other side, Leira, too, had been dreaming of crossing the river. She had often imagined what life was like in the hills, and that same night, she slipped away from her village and made her way to the riverbank."

The villagers of Eldena were quiet, enraptured by the unfolding tale. Lena could feel the anticipation building inside her, wondering what would happen when Milo and Leira finally met.

"As fate would have it," the storyteller said, "Milo and Leira arrived at the riverbank at the same time, each from their own side. They stared at one another in surprise, for they had never seen anyone so different. Milo, tall and sun-bronzed, with his rough hands and broad shoulders, and Leira, small and pale, with her quick fingers and delicate features. For a moment, they simply stood there, uncertain of what to say."

Lena's heart pounded. She could imagine the uncertainty, the way Milo and Leira must have felt as they faced someone so unlike themselves.

"But then," the storyteller continued, his voice softening, "Leira smiled, and Milo smiled back. And in that moment, they knew that despite their differences, they were the same in all the ways that mattered. They were both explorers, both dreamers, both eager to learn about the world and each other."

The villagers sighed softly, the tension in the story giving way to a sense of warmth. Lena felt her own heart swell with joy. Milo and Leira had found a connection, not in their appearances or their backgrounds, but in their shared curiosity and spirit.

"Over the following days," the storyteller said, "Milo and Leira met at the riverbank again and again, learning to communicate through gestures and shared laughter, even though their languages were different. They taught each other their ways—Milo showing Leira how to climb the steep hills, and Leira teaching Milo how to weave intricate patterns with her nimble fingers. Their friendship grew, and soon, the river that had once separated their villages became a place of connection, a bridge between two worlds."

The villagers of Eldena were smiling now, their faces filled with warmth as they imagined the growing bond between Milo and Leira. Lena felt a deep sense of joy in her heart, knowing that friendship could overcome any barrier, even one as vast as a river or as deep as cultural differences.

"But," the storyteller said, his voice turning somber, "not everyone in the villages was pleased. Some of the elders from both sides feared that the friendship between Milo and Leira would upset the balance, that it would lead to the mixing of their ways, their traditions. They worried that the two villages would lose their identities, that they would no longer be distinct."

The mood in the square shifted, a quiet tension settling over the crowd. Lena felt a familiar pang of sadness. She had seen this before—the fear that came when people tried to protect what was familiar, even at the cost of something new and beautiful.

"The elders," the storyteller continued, "tried to forbid Milo and Leira from meeting at the river. They told them that their friendship was dangerous, that they were too different to truly understand one another. But Milo and Leira knew better. They knew that their differences were what made their friendship so special, that by learning from one another, they were becoming stronger, more connected."

Lena's heart raced. She admired Milo and Leira's determination, their refusal to let fear and misunderstanding stand in the way of their friendship.

"And so," the storyteller said, "Milo and Leira continued to meet, even in secret if they had to. They built a small bridge together, one plank at a time, so that they could cross the river whenever they wanted. And as the bridge grew, so did their bond, uniting their villages in ways that no one had thought possible."

The villagers of Eldena were silent, their expressions thoughtful. Lena could see that the story had touched them deeply, that it had reminded them of the power of connection, even in the face of fear and division.

"In time," the storyteller said, "the people of both villages began to see what Milo and Leira had known all along—that their friendship was not a threat, but a gift. They began to cross the bridge themselves, learning from one another, sharing their ways and their traditions. The river that had once divided them became a symbol of unity, a place where differences were celebrated, not feared."

The villagers sat in thoughtful silence, the weight of the story settling over them. Lena felt a deep sense of gratitude, her heart full of hope. Milo and Leira's story had shown her that true friendship wasn't about being the same—it was about embracing each other's differences and finding strength in them.

The storyteller said to the crowd. "Milo and Leira's friendship reminds us that our differences are not something to fear. They are what make us unique, what give us the opportunity to learn from one another. And when we build bridges instead of walls, we create a world where we can all grow stronger together."

Lessons Learned

1. True friendship is built on understanding and acceptance, not sameness.
2. Differences can bring people closer together, creating stronger connections.
3. Fear of losing our identity can prevent us from forming meaningful relationships.
4. Learning from one another enriches both individuals and communities.
5. Building bridges, not walls, fosters unity and growth.
6. Friendship can thrive despite cultural, linguistic, or physical differences.
7. Collaboration and mutual respect can overcome even the deepest divides.
8. Connection is built through shared experiences, even when they seem small.
9. It's important to stand by your friendships, even in the face of opposition.
10. The things that make us different are often the things that make our friendships most valuable.

Chapter 10: The Journey Begins

Lena had always known that her village was small, nestled safely between the mountains, its walls closing in a bit more with each generation. The stories she had heard from the storyteller had stirred something deep within her—a longing that couldn't be ignored. Each tale opened a window to a world she hadn't known existed, and the more stories she heard, the more she felt the need to see these places for herself. The other children in the village loved hearing the stories, but Lena was different. She didn't just want to hear about these lands; she wanted to go to them.

It was late one evening, after the sun had set and the sky had become a blanket of stars, that Lena finally decided she couldn't wait any longer. The village had heard enough stories to begin to open its heart to the world, but she needed to do more. She needed to explore, to learn firsthand, and to bring back stories of her own. Sitting in front of the fire in her family's small home, she shared her thoughts with her parents.

"Mother, Father," she began, her voice steady though her heart pounded in her chest, "I've been thinking for a long time now. I want to go beyond the village. I want to see the world that the storyteller speaks of, and I want to bring back stories of my own."

Her mother's knitting needles stilled in her hands, and her father, who had been repairing a tool, set it down with a heavy sigh. For a long moment, the only sound was the crackle of the fire.

"You're young," her father said finally, his voice filled with concern. "The world outside the village is vast, and there are dangers. You don't know what you might find."

"I know," Lena said quietly, her gaze steady. "But I'm not afraid. I've heard the stories of bravery, of different lands and people, and I want to see them. I want to learn from them. And more than anything, I want to help our village by bringing back the lessons from these stories."

Her mother spoke next, her voice softer but no less serious. "Lena, we've sheltered you here for a reason. The world outside is unknown to us. We've lived in this village for generations, and our people have thrived by staying within its boundaries. Why leave when there's so much safety and comfort here?"

Lena felt a pang of guilt but stood firm. "I love this village, and I know that it has kept us safe. But what if there's more? What if there are stories, like the ones the storyteller brings, that can teach us even more than we know? What if there are places we can't even imagine, full of people and ideas that could help us grow? I don't want to leave forever. I just want to see for myself what's out there, to bring back knowledge that can help us."

Her parents exchanged a long look, filled with concern and something else—perhaps recognition that their daughter had grown in ways they hadn't anticipated.

"We can't stop you," her father said finally, his voice heavy with resignation. "But we worry for your safety. The world is not just filled with wonders; it's filled with dangers too. Will you promise to be careful, to return to us when you can?"

Lena nodded, her heart swelling with gratitude and determination. "I will be careful. And I will come back, I promise. But I have to go."

The next morning, Lena set out with a small bag of supplies—a few pieces of bread, some dried fruit, and a flask of water. Her parents stood at the village gate, watching as she prepared to leave. The sun was just rising, casting long shadows over the village square, and the air was cool with the promise of the day ahead. Other villagers gathered, some curious, others concerned. They knew Lena as the girl who loved stories, but few had expected her to take such a bold step.

The storyteller himself was there, leaning against his horse, his eyes twinkling with pride. He approached Lena just as she was about to step beyond the village gate.

"You're brave," he said with a smile, "and curious. Those are the best traits for a storyteller. But remember, the world is not always as it seems. Be ready for surprises, both good and bad. And trust in your heart, for it will guide you."

Lena nodded, her resolve firm. "I'll be careful, and I'll come back with stories to share."

With a final wave to her parents and the villagers, Lena stepped beyond the gate and into the world beyond. It felt strange at first, the open expanse of the fields stretching out before her, the mountains in the distance like silent guardians. She had never ventured far from the village, and now, every step took her farther from the only home she had ever known.

As she walked, Lena thought about the stories she had heard. She imagined the desert lands of Nia, the quiet strength of Kian, the bravery of Liora, and the vibrant colors of Zaria's world. Each story was like a thread, weaving a tapestry that stretched far beyond the borders of her village. She wanted to be a part of that tapestry, to add her own stories to it.

The first day of her journey was peaceful, the path clear and the weather mild. Lena walked steadily, her heart filled with excitement and curiosity. By evening, she found a small grove of trees where she could rest for the night. She ate some of the bread her mother had packed for her, the taste familiar and comforting. As the sun set, casting the sky in hues of pink and orange, Lena felt a sense of calm wash over her. She was on her way, and though the path ahead was uncertain, she knew she was doing the right thing.

The next morning, Lena woke early and continued on her journey. The landscape began to change as she traveled farther from the village. The fields gave way to rolling hills, and the air grew cooler as she ascended into higher terrain. By midday, she found herself standing on a ridge, looking out over a valley below. It was breathtaking—the valley was lush and green, dotted with flowers of every color, and a sparkling river wound its way through the center. Lena smiled to herself, knowing that she had found something beautiful, something she had never seen before.

As she descended into the valley, Lena marveled at the vibrant life around her. Birds sang in the trees, and the air was filled with the sweet scent of blooming flowers. She knelt by the river, cupping her hands to drink the cool, clear water. It was refreshing, and she felt a surge of energy as she stood and continued on her way.

Lena found herself growing tired. The path through the valley was longer than she had expected, and her feet ached from the hours of walking. She glanced up at the sky, where dark clouds were beginning to gather. The air had grown heavy, and Lena knew that a storm was coming.

She quickened her pace, hoping to find shelter before the rain began. But as she pressed on, the wind picked up, and soon, fat drops of rain began to fall. Lena pulled her cloak tighter around her, searching desperately for a place to take cover. In the distance, she saw the outline of a small building—a cottage, perhaps—and she hurried toward it.

By the time she reached the cottage, the rain was pouring down in sheets, and thunder rumbled overhead. Lena knocked on the door, hoping that whoever lived there would offer her shelter for the night.

The door creaked open, and an elderly woman peered out at Lena, her eyes sharp and inquisitive. "What brings you here, child?" the woman asked, her voice rough but not unkind.

"I'm traveling," Lena replied, her voice slightly breathless from the exertion. "I'm from the village of Eldena, and I'm on a journey to learn more about the world. The storm caught me by surprise, and I was hoping for shelter."

The woman's eyes softened, and she nodded. "Come in, then. You're welcome to stay until the storm passes."

Lena stepped inside, grateful for the warmth of the cottage. The interior was small but cozy, with a fire crackling in the hearth and a simple table set with bread and cheese. The woman gestured for Lena to sit, and she did so, warming her hands by the fire.

Lessons Learned

1. Curiosity can lead to new experiences and growth.
2. Stepping outside of one's comfort zone is the first step toward discovery.
3. The world is full of beauty, but it is also full of challenges.
4. Courage is not the absence of fear, but the willingness to move forward despite it.
5. Change is often met with resistance, but it is necessary for growth.
6. Traveling the unknown path teaches us about ourselves and the world around us.
7. Every new experience is a story waiting to be told.
8. The kindness of strangers can be a light in the face of uncertainty.
9. Not every lesson will be easy, but each one is valuable.
10. Journeys, whether physical or emotional, are filled with surprises and opportunities for growth.

Chapter 11: The Village of Many Languages

After the storm passed, Lena bid farewell to Annis, feeling a renewed sense of purpose. The elderly woman had offered her more than just shelter from the rain—she had shared wisdom, hinting at the challenges ahead, but also encouraging Lena to keep moving forward. The road ahead would be filled with both wonder and difficulty, and Lena knew she had to embrace both to fulfill her journey.

As the sun rose higher in the sky, Lena walked through the valley, marveling at the beauty around her. Birds flitted between the trees, and the river continued to wind its way through the landscape, sparkling in the morning light. She felt a sense of freedom, a connection to the land that was different from what she had known in Eldena. But as much as she enjoyed the solitude of her journey, Lena couldn't help but wonder about the people she might meet in the days ahead. The stories she had heard from the storyteller had taught her that the world was full of diverse cultures, and she longed to experience them firsthand.

It wasn't long before her path led her to the edge of a new village. Unlike Eldena, this village was lively and bustling, with people moving quickly through the streets, carrying baskets of goods and chatting animatedly with one another. But what struck Lena the most was the sound. Everywhere she turned, people were speaking, but not in the same language. The air was filled with a cacophony of voices, each one distinct, each one beautiful in its own way.

Lena paused at the edge of the village, her heart pounding with excitement. She had never encountered anything like this before. In Eldena, everyone spoke the same language, their words familiar and comforting. But here, in this village, the words were foreign, unfamiliar, yet somehow inviting. It was as if the very air was alive with the music of speech, and Lena couldn't wait to learn more.

She took a deep breath and stepped into the village, her eyes wide with curiosity. The people around her were friendly, smiling at her as she passed, though she couldn't understand what they were saying. For the first time, Lena felt the weight of her own ignorance. She had always taken for granted that she could communicate with the people around her, but now, in this village of many languages, she realized that there was so much she didn't know.

As she wandered through the streets, Lena came across a group of children playing in a courtyard. They were laughing and chasing each other, their voices a blend of different languages. One of the children, a girl about Lena's age, noticed her and waved her over. Lena hesitated for a moment, unsure of how to communicate, but the girl's smile was warm and inviting.

"Come, join us!" the girl said, her accent thick but her meaning clear. Lena's eyes widened in surprise. She understood! The girl spoke her language, though it sounded different, as if shaped by a different world. Grateful for the familiar words, Lena smiled and joined the children in their game, her heart light with relief.

After the game ended, the girl introduced herself as Zara. "You're not from here, are you?" Zara asked, her eyes sparkling with curiosity. "I can tell by the way you look around. This village is new to you."

Lena nodded, laughing softly. "Yes, I'm from Eldena. It's a small village, not too far from here. But everyone there speaks the same language. I've never been to a place like this, where everyone speaks so many different words."

Zara grinned. "It can be confusing at first, but it's wonderful too. Here, we have people from all over, each with their own language and way of speaking. Some have come from distant lands, others from nearby villages. We've learned to understand each other, even though our words are different."

Lena marveled at Zara's words. "How do you do it?" she asked. "How do you understand each other when everyone speaks differently?"

Zara's smile widened. "We learn. We listen. And sometimes, when the words don't work, we use our hands, our faces, our hearts. There are so many ways to communicate, if you're willing to try."

Lena nodded thoughtfully, her mind racing. She had never considered that communication could be more than just words. In Eldena, everyone had always spoken the same language, and words were the primary means of connection. But here, in this village, there was a richness to communication that went beyond language. It was about understanding one another, not just through words, but through gestures, expressions, and the simple willingness to listen.

As the day wore on, Zara showed Lena around the village, introducing her to the people who lived there. Each time they met someone new, Lena heard a different language, a different rhythm to the speech. Some were soft and melodic, others quick and sharp. But no matter how different the words were, the people always found a way to connect.

At one point, they visited a bustling market where vendors called out in languages Lena didn't understand, their voices mingling in the air like a symphony. Lena watched as Zara effortlessly switched between languages, speaking to each vendor in their own tongue, while using gestures and facial expressions to bridge any gaps in understanding. It was fascinating to watch, and Lena felt a deep admiration for the way the villagers navigated this complex web of communication with such ease.

By the time evening fell, Lena had learned a few words from different languages—simple phrases like "hello," "thank you," and "goodbye." Though her knowledge was still limited, she felt a sense of accomplishment. It wasn't just about learning new words; it was about understanding that language was more than just a means of communication. It was a bridge between people, a way to connect across differences and find common ground.

As they sat by a fire that night, Zara and Lena shared stories of their villages. Lena spoke of Eldena, of its traditions and the stories the storyteller had brought. Zara, in turn, told Lena about her own village's history—how people from all over had come to settle there, each bringing their own language and customs. It hadn't always been easy, Zara explained. At first, there had been misunderstandings, frustrations over not being able to communicate. But over time, the villagers had learned to listen more closely, to be patient with one another, and to embrace the beauty of their differences.

"We're all different," Zara said, her voice soft and thoughtful, "but in the end, we're the same too. We want to be understood, to connect, to belong. And when we make the effort to understand each other, we find that we're not so different after all."

Lena smiled, feeling a deep sense of connection with Zara. They came from different places, spoke different languages, but in that moment, it didn't matter. They understood each other, not just through words, but through the shared experience of wanting to explore the world, to learn from it, and to bring those lessons back home.

As Lena lay down to sleep that night, her mind was filled with thoughts of the day. She had learned so much in such a short time—about language, about communication, and about the power of understanding. The village of many languages had shown her that the world was full of different ways to connect, and that with patience and an open heart, anyone could find a way to bridge the gaps between them.

The next morning, Lena woke early, ready to continue her journey. As she prepared to leave, Zara met her at the edge of the village, her smile warm and bright.

"Thank you," Lena said, her voice filled with gratitude. "You've taught me so much, and I'll never forget it."

Zara grinned. "And you've taught me too. It's always good to see the world through someone else's eyes. Safe travels, Lena. And remember—no matter where you go, you'll always find a way to connect."

With a final wave, Lena set off, her heart full of the lessons she had learned in the village of many languages. She knew that the road ahead would bring more challenges, more discoveries, but she was ready for them. Each step took her closer to new stories, new people, and new ways of understanding the world.

Lessons Learned

1. Language is a bridge that connects people across differences.
2. Communication is not just about words; it's about gestures, expressions, and understanding.
3. Patience and a willingness to listen are key to understanding others.
4. Cultural differences enrich communities and bring people closer together.
5. Learning new languages opens doors to new friendships and connections.
6. Even in the face of language barriers, people can find ways to communicate and understand each other.
7. There is beauty in diversity, and each language brings its own rhythm and music to the world.
8. Connection is a universal need, and with effort, we can find common ground with anyone.
9. Differences should be embraced, as they make our interactions richer and more meaningful.
10. No matter where we come from or what language we speak, we all share the same desire to connect and belong.

Chapter 12: A Tale of the Mountain People

Lena's journey had taken her through valleys, forests, and bustling villages, each place offering its own lessons and stories. But as she continued her travels, she found herself drawn to the towering mountains in the distance. They loomed over the horizon, their peaks covered in snow, their slopes dark and mysterious. The mountains seemed like a world apart, isolated and distant from the lands below, and Lena's heart raced with curiosity. What kind of people lived in such a harsh and unforgiving place? What stories did they have to tell?

Determined to find out, Lena set her sights on the mountains. The journey was long and arduous, the path winding steeply upward through rocky terrain. As she climbed higher, the air grew colder, and the trees became sparse, giving way to rugged cliffs and jagged rocks. But despite the difficulty, Lena pressed on, her heart filled with excitement at the thought of discovering a new place, a new world.

After several days of climbing, Lena finally reached a small village nestled on a high plateau, surrounded by towering cliffs. The village was unlike anything she had seen before. The houses were built from stone, their roofs low and sloped to protect against the heavy snow that must fall during the winter months. The people, too, were different—strong and sturdy, with weathered faces and thick, woolen clothes to guard against the cold.

As Lena entered the village, she was greeted by curious glances. The people here were not used to strangers, especially not ones from the lowlands. But there was no hostility in their eyes, only curiosity. A few of the children ran to get the elders, and soon Lena found herself standing before the village chief, a tall man with a grizzled beard and kind eyes.

"Welcome, traveler," the chief said in a deep, resonant voice. "It is rare for us to have visitors, especially from the lands below. What brings you to our mountain?"

Lena smiled, bowing her head respectfully. "I've come to learn," she said simply. "I've been traveling from village to village, listening to stories and learning about the people and places I encounter. I've heard stories of these mountains, and I wanted to see them for myself."

The chief nodded, his expression thoughtful. "You are brave to come so far. The mountains are not kind to those who are unprepared. But you are welcome here, and if it is stories you seek, we have many to share."

Lena felt a surge of gratitude. She had come seeking knowledge, and it seemed she had found it. The villagers invited her to stay, offering her a place to rest and food to eat. As she sat by the fire that evening, wrapped in a thick blanket to ward off the chill, the chief and the elders gathered around her, ready to share their tales.

The first story the chief told was one of survival—a tale that spoke to the harsh realities of life in the mountains. He spoke of the great winter that had struck the village many years ago, a winter so fierce that the snow piled higher than the roofs of the houses, and the winds howled day and night without end. The villagers had been trapped, unable to leave their homes, their food supplies running dangerously low.

"But we did not give up," the chief said, his voice steady and calm. "We knew that survival in the mountains meant relying on one another, on our strength and our will to endure. The elders taught the younger ones how to conserve their energy, how to stretch the smallest amount of food to last as long as possible. We rationed, we shared, and most importantly, we did not lose hope."

Lena listened intently, feeling a deep respect for the resilience of the mountain people. They had faced challenges that many in the lowlands would never encounter, yet they had not been defeated. They had found ways to survive, to thrive even in the face of adversity.

"But survival is not enough," the chief continued. "To live in the mountains is to understand that the land gives as much as it takes. We learned to read the signs of nature—the way the wind changes before a storm, the way the animals behave before the first snowfall. We learned that the mountains are not our enemies, but our teachers. They test us, yes, but they also reward us with knowledge, with wisdom."

The other elders nodded in agreement, their eyes shining with pride. Lena could see that the mountains were more than just a place to live for these people. They were a part of their identity, shaping their lives in ways that those who lived below could never truly understand.

As the night wore on, the chief shared more stories—tales of the great hunts, of the festivals that celebrated the changing of the seasons, of the bonds that held the village together through the hardest of times. Each story was filled with lessons, not just about survival, but about the importance of community, of trust, of understanding the land and its rhythms.

Lena was captivated by the stories, but what struck her most was the deep sense of connection the villagers had to their home. The mountains, with all their challenges and dangers, were not seen as something to fear or escape from. They were seen as a source of strength, a reminder that life was not always easy, but that it was always worth fighting for.

Lena thanked the chief and the villagers, her heart full of gratitude for the stories they had shared. As she descended the mountain, the stone clutched in her hand, she reflected on what she had learned. The mountains were more than just a place of beauty or danger—they were a place of wisdom, where the harshest conditions could teach the most valuable lessons.

Lessons Learned

1. Resilience is key to overcoming challenges, no matter how great they seem.
2. Survival is not just about strength, but about knowledge and adaptability.

3. Nature, even in its harshest forms, can be a teacher if we are willing to listen.
4. Community and cooperation are essential to enduring difficult times.
5. Every environment, no matter how tough, offers its own rewards and wisdom.
6. Hope is the light that keeps us going when everything else seems lost.
7. The land we live on shapes who we are and how we live our lives.
8. Strength comes from within, but it is also drawn from the world around us.
9. The challenges we face often teach us the most valuable lessons.
10. Adversity can be a source of growth and transformation if we embrace it.

Chapter 13: The Story of the Tiny Elephant

The landscape changed once again as Lena left the mountains behind, her path now leading her through lush, green forests. The air was warmer here, filled with the scent of pine and wildflowers, and the sound of birdsong accompanied her as she walked. It was a welcome change from the cold and rugged terrain of the mountains, and Lena felt a sense of lightness in her step as she continued her journey.

As she traveled deeper into the forest, Lena began to notice signs of another village. The trees thinned slightly, revealing small paths worn into the ground by the feet of travelers, and in the distance, she could see the faint outline of rooftops peeking through the canopy. Curious, Lena quickened her pace, eager to see what this new village had to offer.

When she arrived, she found a bustling community, filled with people going about their daily lives. Children ran through the streets, laughing and playing, while adults worked in the fields or tended to their shops. It was a peaceful, happy place, and Lena felt immediately at ease.

As she wandered through the village, admiring the brightly painted houses and the colorful market stalls, Lena overheard a group of children talking excitedly about something. They were huddled together near a fountain, their voices filled with awe and excitement.

"It's true!" one of the children exclaimed. "My grandfather told me the story himself. The tiny elephant saved the entire village!"

Lena's ears perked up at the mention of a tiny elephant. She had never heard of such a creature, and her curiosity got the better of her. She approached the group of children, smiling warmly.

"Excuse me," she said, "did you say something about a tiny elephant? What's the story?"

The children turned to her, their eyes wide with excitement. "You haven't heard the story of the tiny elephant?" one of the boys asked, clearly surprised. "It's one of the most famous stories in our village!"

Lena shook her head, her curiosity growing. "No, I haven't. But I'd love to hear it."

The children exchanged excited glances before one of the girls, the oldest of the group, stepped forward. "I'll tell you the story," she said, her voice full of pride. "It's a story that's been passed down for generations, and it's about a very special elephant."

Lena smiled and settled onto a nearby bench, eager to hear the tale.

"Many years ago," the girl began, "there was a terrible drought in our village. The rivers dried up, the crops withered in the fields, and the animals left in search of water. The people of the village were desperate. Without water, they couldn't survive. The elders called a meeting to figure out what to do, but no one had a solution."

Lena leaned forward, already captivated by the story.

"But then," the girl continued, her eyes shining with excitement, "something amazing happened. One of the villagers, a man who worked in the fields, came running into the square, shouting that he had found something. Everyone gathered around to see what it was, and there, standing beside him, was a tiny elephant."

The children giggled at the thought of such a creature, and Lena smiled. She could picture it in her mind—a tiny elephant, no bigger than a goat, standing in the middle of the village square.

"The people couldn't believe their eyes," the girl said. "They had never seen such a small elephant before. It was only about as tall as a man's knee, but it was perfectly formed, with big ears and a long trunk, just like a regular elephant. The man told the villagers that he had found the elephant near the dried-up riverbed, and that it had been digging in the dirt with its trunk."

Lena listened intently, her imagination running wild. She had heard stories of elephants before, but never of one so small. What could this tiny creature do to help the village?

"At first," the girl said, her voice growing softer, "the people didn't think much of the tiny elephant. It was too small to be of any use, they thought. But the man who had found it insisted that they give the elephant a chance. He believed that the elephant had come to help them, even though it was so small."

The villagers in the story were doubtful, Lena could tell, but she admired the man's faith in the tiny elephant. Sometimes, it took someone with vision to see the potential in something others overlooked.

"The villagers decided to let the tiny elephant stay," the girl continued, "and every day, it would go down to the riverbed and dig in the dirt with its trunk. At first, nothing happened. The ground was dry and hard, and there was no sign of water. But the tiny elephant didn't give up. It kept digging, day after day, even when the other animals and people had given up hope."

Lena felt a sense of admiration for the tiny elephant. Despite its size, it was determined to help, to keep working even when the odds were against it.

"And then," the girl said, her voice filled with excitement, "after many days of digging, something amazing happened. The tiny elephant struck water! A small trickle of water began to flow from the ground, and soon, it grew into a stream. The villagers were overjoyed! The drought was over, and the tiny elephant had saved them all."

The children clapped and cheered, clearly proud of their village's story. Lena couldn't help but smile, her heart full of warmth. The story of the tiny elephant was more than just a tale of survival—it was a reminder that even the smallest, most overlooked creatures could make a difference.

"The tiny elephant became a hero in our village," the girl said, her voice soft with reverence. "And ever since then, we've honored it by telling its story. It reminds us that no matter how small or insignificant something may seem, it can still have a great impact."

As the children finished their story, Lena thanked them, her heart full of gratitude for the tale they had shared. The story of the tiny elephant had touched her deeply, and she knew that it was a lesson she would carry with her for the rest of her journey.

Lena reflected on her own journey. She was just one person, traveling alone through a vast and unfamiliar world. At times, she had felt small and insignificant, unsure of what difference she could make. But the story of the tiny elephant reminded her that size didn't matter—what mattered was the heart, the will to keep going, even when things seemed impossible.

Lessons Learned

1. Even the smallest among us can make a big difference.
2. Determination and perseverance are more important than size or strength.
3. It's easy to overlook small things, but they often hold great value.
4. Faith in the seemingly impossible can lead to extraordinary outcomes.
5. Heroes come in all shapes and sizes, and their impact isn't determined by how they look.
6. Success often comes from refusing to give up, even when the odds seem insurmountable.
7. Community support can be built by believing in the potential of every individual, no matter how small.
8. Hope can be found in the most unexpected places.
9. Believing in yourself and your abilities is key to overcoming challenges.
10. Sometimes the greatest strength lies in quiet persistence rather than grand gestures.

Chapter 14: The City of Inventors

Lena's journey had taken her across valleys and through forests, over mountains and through villages that had broadened her understanding of the world. Each place she visited taught her something new about the diversity of people, their customs, and their ways of thinking. But as she continued on her way, she began to hear whispers of a place that seemed unlike any other: a city of inventors, where creativity and innovation were at the heart of everything.

The stories spoke of a city where people built marvelous machines, where ideas flowed as freely as rivers, and where the boundaries of possibility were constantly being pushed. Lena had always been curious, but hearing about such a place sparked something new inside her. She had seen so many different ways of life, but she had never encountered a place where invention itself was celebrated, where people were encouraged to dream up the impossible and make it real.

Determined to see the city for herself, Lena set off once again, her steps quickened by excitement. The road to the city of inventors was long, winding through a mixture of lush forests and wide-open plains. But eventually, after several days of travel, Lena saw it in the distance—a sprawling city, gleaming with the light of countless inventions. The skyline was unlike anything she had ever seen before, dotted with towering structures made of metal and glass, their shapes twisting and spiraling into the sky.

As Lena approached the city gates, she was greeted by the sound of humming machinery, the clatter of tools, and the excited chatter of people at work. The air itself seemed to buzz with energy, as if the very atmosphere was charged with the creative spirit of the inventors who lived there.

Lena's eyes widened as she entered the city. Everywhere she looked, there were people building, crafting, and testing new inventions. In one corner, a group of children tinkered with a machine that could send messages across great distances. In another, an elderly man carefully adjusted the gears of a clock that could tell not just the time, but the phases of the moon and the changing of the tides.

The people of the city moved with purpose, their hands busy, their minds clearly filled with ideas. And yet, there was a lightness to the way they worked, as if invention itself brought them joy. Lena wandered through the streets, marveling at the creativity and ingenuity on display.

Eventually, she came across a group of inventors gathered around a large table in the middle of a public square. They were deep in discussion, their hands moving as they sketched designs and shared ideas. One of them, a young woman with bright eyes and oil-smeared hands, noticed Lena watching from a distance and waved her over.

"Come, join us!" the woman called out, her voice filled with excitement. "You're just in time. We're working on something new, and we could use some fresh ideas."

Lena hesitated for a moment, unsure of what she could contribute to such an intelligent and creative group. But the woman's enthusiasm was infectious, and soon Lena found herself seated at the table, watching as the inventors explained their latest project.

"We're trying to build a machine that can help with farming," the young woman explained, her hands gesturing animatedly as she spoke. "The idea is to create something that can water crops automatically, so farmers can focus on other tasks. But we're stuck on how to make the machine smart enough to know when the plants need water."

Lena listened intently, her mind racing with the possibilities. She wasn't an inventor, but she had spent enough time traveling to understand that every problem had a solution if you looked at it from the right angle. "What if," she suggested cautiously, "you use the soil itself to help the machine decide? If the soil is dry, maybe the machine could sense that and know it's time to water."

The group of inventors fell silent for a moment, considering Lena's idea. Then, the young woman's face lit up with a wide smile. "That's brilliant!" she exclaimed. "Why didn't we think of that before? Using the soil as a guide... it's so simple, but it could work!"

Excitement rippled through the group, and soon they were sketching out new designs, incorporating Lena's idea into their plans. Lena watched in awe as the inventors worked, their minds moving quickly from one idea to the next, each building on the other until a new invention began to take shape.

As the day wore on, Lena found herself completely absorbed in the world of invention. She didn't have the technical skills of the inventors, but her time spent traveling and learning had given her a unique perspective. She offered ideas when she could, drawing on the lessons she had learned from the people she had met. And the inventors, eager to explore new possibilities, welcomed her contributions with open arms.

By the time the sun began to set, the group had made significant progress on their machine. They weren't finished yet, but they were closer than they had been when Lena first arrived. As they packed up their tools for the night, the young woman turned to Lena, her eyes filled with gratitude.

"Thank you," she said earnestly. "You may not be an inventor in the traditional sense, but your ideas helped us see things differently. That's what this city is all about—finding new ways to look at the world and using that perspective to create something amazing."

Lena smiled, her heart full of warmth. "I'm glad I could help," she said. "This city is incredible. I've never seen anything like it."

The young woman laughed. "That's the beauty of invention," she said. "It's about imagining something that doesn't exist yet and then making it real. And everyone, no matter where they come from, can contribute to that process. You don't have to be an expert—you just have to be willing to think differently."

Lena spent the next few days in the city, learning from the inventors and watching as they brought their ideas to life. She marveled at their creativity, their determination, and their willingness to fail and try again. In the city of inventors, failure wasn't seen as something to be feared—it was simply a step along the path to success. Each mistake was an opportunity to learn, to improve, and to create something even better.

Lessons Learned

1. Creativity is not limited to experts; anyone can contribute ideas that spark innovation.
2. Invention is about seeing the world differently and imagining what could be.
3. Failure is a natural part of the creative process and should be embraced as an opportunity to learn.
4. Collaboration and sharing ideas lead to greater innovation than working in isolation.
5. Problem-solving requires looking at challenges from multiple perspectives.
6. Ingenuity and creativity are tools for making the impossible possible.
7. Thinking outside the box opens the door to new possibilities.
8. Persistence is key in the invention process—each failure brings you closer to success.
9. The willingness to explore new ideas is the heart of progress.
10. Everyone has the potential to be creative and inventive if they embrace new ways of thinking.

Chapter 15: The Tale of the Dancing Birds

The city of inventors had left Lena with a sense of wonder and possibility, but as she continued her journey, she found herself longing for something different. The mechanical wonders of the city were inspiring, but Lena had always been drawn to the natural world as well, to the rhythms and patterns of life that seemed to move in ways no invention could replicate.

It was this desire to reconnect with nature that led Lena to a place she had heard whispers of on her travels—a land where the people lived in harmony with the birds, a place where music and dance were not just forms of entertainment, but ways of communicating with the world around them. The stories described it as a place of beauty and grace, where the birds danced in the sky and the people followed their lead, moving together in perfect rhythm.

The idea fascinated Lena. She had always loved music and movement, but the thought of a people who communicated through dance, who learned from the birds themselves, was something she had never imagined. And so, with her curiosity guiding her once again, Lena set off for this fabled land.

The journey took her through dense forests and over gentle hills, and as she traveled, she began to notice something unusual. The birds she encountered along the way seemed to move differently here. Their wings beat in time with the wind, their calls echoed in perfect harmony with the rustling of the trees. It was as if the entire world had become a symphony, with every creature playing its part.

After several days of travel, Lena finally arrived at the village she had been seeking. It was a small, peaceful place, nestled in a valley surrounded by towering trees. The houses were simple, made of wood and thatch, and everywhere Lena looked, she saw birds—perched on rooftops, flitting between branches, and soaring high in the sky above.

As Lena entered the village, she was greeted by a young woman who moved with such grace that it seemed as though she was dancing even as she walked. Her name was Suri, and she welcomed Lena with a warm smile.

"You've come at a special time," Suri said, her voice light and melodic. "The Festival of the Birds is about to begin. It's a time of celebration, when we honor the birds and the gifts they bring us."

Lena's heart swelled with excitement. "What is the festival like?" she asked.

Suri's eyes sparkled with joy. "It's a time for dancing, for singing, for becoming one with the world around us. The birds lead the way, and we follow, moving in harmony with them. It's a reminder that we are all connected, that every creature has its own rhythm, its own dance."

Lena smiled, her excitement growing. She had never experienced anything like this before, and she couldn't wait to see the festival for herself.

That evening, as the sun began to set, the entire village gathered in a large clearing at the edge of the forest. The air was filled with anticipation, and Lena could feel the energy building around her. Suri stood by her side, her eyes fixed on the sky above.

"Watch," Suri whispered, her voice barely audible. "They're coming."

Lena followed Suri's gaze, her breath catching in her throat as she saw the first of the birds appear. They came from all directions, their wings glowing in the fading light of the sun. There were birds of every size and color—some with bright, iridescent feathers that shimmered like jewels, others with wings so large that they cast shadows over the ground below.

As the birds circled overhead, their movements became more synchronized, more deliberate. They weren't just flying—they were dancing. Their wings beat in time with an invisible rhythm, their patterns weaving together in a breathtaking display of grace and beauty.

And then, as if on cue, the people of the village began to move. They stepped into the clearing, their bodies swaying in time with the birds above. The dance was slow at first, gentle and fluid, but as the birds' movements became more intricate, so too did the dance of the people. Their feet moved faster, their arms lifted higher, and soon the entire clearing was alive with motion, with the rhythm of the birds and the people moving as one.

Lena stood at the edge of the clearing, her heart pounding in time with the beat of the dance. She had never seen anything so beautiful, so perfectly in harmony. It was as if the line between the earth and the sky had disappeared, and for a moment, all of nature was connected in a single, flowing movement.

Suri, noticing Lena's awe, took her by the hand. "Come," she said, her smile wide and welcoming. "Join us."

Lena hesitated for only a moment before stepping into the clearing. She had never danced like this before, but as she moved, she realized that it wasn't about knowing the steps or getting the movements exactly right. It was about feeling the rhythm, about letting the music of the birds and the earth guide her.

As Lena danced, she felt a sense of freedom unlike anything she had ever experienced. The worries of the world faded away, and for the first time in her life, she felt completely in tune with the world around her. The birds soared overhead, their wings beating in perfect time with the movements of the people below, and Lena knew that she was part of something much larger than herself.

The festival continued late into the night, the sky filled with stars and the air alive with the sound of birdsong and laughter. Lena danced until her feet ached and her heart felt full to bursting. And when the night finally ended, and the birds began to disappear into the forest once more, Lena found herself standing at the edge of the clearing, her heart filled with gratitude.

Suri approached her, her own face flushed with the joy of the dance. "You danced beautifully," she said softly. "You understand now, don't you? The dance isn't just about movement. It's about connection—about being part of the world, of nature, of everything around us."

Lena nodded, her heart still racing from the experience. "I've never felt anything like it," she admitted. "It's like I became part of the rhythm of the earth itself."

Suri smiled. "That's the gift the birds bring us. They remind us that we are all connected, that every creature, every person, has their own rhythm, their own dance. And when we move together, we create something beautiful."

Lena spent the next few days in the village, learning more about the people's way of life. They lived simply, but their connection to the natural world was profound. Every day, they danced with the birds, their movements a reflection of the rhythms they saw in the world around them. It wasn't just a festival tradition—it was a way of life, a reminder that they were part of a larger whole.

By the time Lena was ready to leave, she had learned more than she ever expected. The village had shown her that connection didn't just come through words or inventions—it could come through movement, through the simple act of being in tune with the world around you. The people of the village had found a way to communicate with the birds, to dance with them, and in doing so, they had discovered a deeper connection to the earth and to each other.

As Lena said her goodbyes to Suri and the other villagers, she felt a sense of peace wash over her. The world was full of different ways to connect, to communicate, to express oneself. And while each place she visited had its own unique customs and traditions, they all shared the same desire—to belong, to be part of something greater.

Lena knew that the lessons she had learned from the village of the dancing birds would stay with her for the rest of her life. She had discovered that the world was full of beauty, of rhythm, of connection, and that sometimes, the most powerful way to communicate was through the simple act of moving in harmony with the world around you.

Lessons Learned

1. Connection to the natural world can bring a deep sense of peace and harmony.
2. Communication isn't limited to words—music, dance, and movement can express powerful emotions.
3. Living in harmony with nature allows us to find balance and joy in everyday life.
4. The rhythms of the earth and its creatures can teach us how to move through life with grace.
5. Every person and creature has their own rhythm, and when we move together, we create something beautiful.
6. Dance is a universal language that can connect people across cultures and traditions.
7. Being in tune with the world around us helps us find our place within it.
8. Nature has its own wisdom, and by observing and listening, we can learn valuable lessons.
9. Festivals and celebrations can be a way to honor the connections we share with others and with the world.
10. True joy comes from being present in the moment, from letting go of our worries and becoming part of the rhythm of life.

Chapter 16: The Secret of the Silent Forest

As Lena continued her journey, the stories she had collected began to fill her mind like pages in a book, each one etched with the lessons she had learned from the people she met. But despite everything she had experienced, she knew that her journey was far from over. Each step she took brought her closer to new lands, new stories, and new understandings of the world. It was this unquenchable thirst for knowledge and discovery that led her to the edge of the Silent Forest, a place she had only heard whispered about in the stories of travelers.

The Silent Forest was said to be a place of deep mystery, where no birds sang and the wind itself seemed to hold its breath. It was a place where the trees stood taller and closer together than in any other forest, their branches intertwined in a way that blocked out even the brightest sunlight. Many believed the forest was enchanted, and that those who entered it never returned. Others said it was simply a place where nature had grown too dense for even sound to penetrate.

Lena stood at the edge of the forest, the dense trees looming before her like silent sentinels. The air around her was unnaturally still, and as she took her first step into the forest, she felt a shiver run down her spine. There were no sounds—not a single birdcall, not even the rustle of leaves. It was as if the entire forest was waiting, holding its breath, as if watching her every move.

Despite the eerie silence, Lena pressed on, her curiosity urging her forward. She had faced many challenges on her journey, and she had learned that even the most mysterious places held stories worth discovering. If the Silent Forest held a secret, Lena was determined to uncover it.

As she walked deeper into the forest, the trees closed in around her, their thick trunks and gnarled branches creating a labyrinth of wood and shadow. The light grew dimmer, and Lena found herself straining to see the path ahead. But despite the darkness, she continued on, her heart steady with determination.

After what felt like hours, Lena finally came upon a small clearing in the heart of the forest. In the center of the clearing stood a single tree, taller and grander than any she had ever seen. Its bark was silver, shimmering faintly in the dim light, and its branches stretched out like arms, reaching toward the sky.

Lena approached the tree cautiously, her heart pounding in her chest. There was something different about this tree—something ancient, as if it had been standing there for centuries, watching over the forest in silence. As she neared the tree, she noticed something even more unusual. Carved into the bark were strange symbols, symbols that seemed to pulse with an energy all their own.

Lena reached out to touch the bark, her fingers brushing against the smooth surface. The moment her skin made contact with the tree, she felt a surge of warmth run through her body, as if the tree itself was alive with power. And then, to her astonishment, she heard a voice.

"Welcome, traveler," the voice said, soft but clear, as if it were speaking directly into her mind. "You have come far, and you have been brave to enter this forest. But do you know why you are here?"

Lena's breath caught in her throat. She had never heard anything like this before—a voice that seemed to come from nowhere and everywhere all at once. She took a deep breath, gathering her thoughts before responding.

"I came because I wanted to learn," she said softly, her voice steady despite the strangeness of the situation. "I've heard stories about this forest, and I wanted to discover its secrets for myself."

The tree seemed to hum in response, its branches swaying slightly as if in approval. "There are many secrets in this world," the voice said, "and not all of them can be spoken aloud. This forest holds one such secret, a story that can only be understood in silence."

Lena frowned slightly, unsure of what the voice meant. "How can a story be told without words?" she asked.

The voice chuckled softly, the sound like the rustling of leaves in the wind. "Not all stories are told with words, traveler. Some are written in the spaces between them. The Silent Forest is a place of stillness, of reflection. It teaches those who enter it the value of listening—not to sounds, but to the silence itself. In silence, we find answers that words cannot provide."

Lena stood still, absorbing the words. She had learned so much on her journey—about people, about cultures, about the power of stories. But she had never considered silence itself to be a storyteller. As she stood there, surrounded by the stillness of the forest, she realized that there was a kind of peace here, a calm that allowed her to reflect on everything she had learned.

"Every traveler who enters this forest does so for a reason," the voice continued. "You seek understanding, but to truly understand, you must first listen. Listen not just to the world around you, but to yourself."

Lena closed her eyes, letting the silence wash over her. In the absence of sound, she began to hear things she hadn't noticed before—the steady rhythm of her own heartbeat, the soft rustle of her breath. And deeper still, she could feel the weight of all the stories she had collected on her journey, each one a part of her now, shaping her in ways she hadn't fully realized.

The silence wasn't empty. It was full—full of meaning, full of possibility. It was a space for reflection, for understanding, for growth. And in that moment, Lena understood the lesson of the Silent Forest.

When she opened her eyes, the tree seemed to shimmer with approval. "You are ready," the voice said softly. "You have listened, and now you understand. The story of the Silent Forest is one of stillness, of patience, of listening to the things that cannot be spoken. Take this lesson with you on your journey, and you will find that the answers you seek are often found in the quietest of places."

Lena nodded, her heart filled with gratitude. She had learned many things on her journey, but the lesson of the Silent Forest was one she knew she would carry with her for the rest of her life. It was a reminder that not all knowledge came from words or actions—sometimes, the most important lessons came from the spaces in between, from the quiet moments of reflection and understanding.

As Lena left the clearing and made her way back through the forest, the stillness no longer felt eerie or strange. Instead, it felt comforting, like a gentle reminder to slow down and listen to the world around her. And as she stepped out of the forest and back into the light of the outside world, she knew that she had gained something invaluable.

The Silent Forest had given her the gift of stillness, the ability to listen to the world in a way she hadn't before. And with that gift, Lena continued her journey, ready to face whatever lay ahead with a new sense of calm and understanding.

Lessons Learned

1. Silence is not empty—it is full of meaning and possibility.
2. Listening is a skill that requires patience and reflection.
3. Not all stories are told with words; some are found in the spaces between.
4. The most important answers often come in moments of stillness.
5. Reflection allows us to understand ourselves and the world more deeply.
6. Peace can be found in quiet moments, away from the noise of the world.
7. Understanding comes not just from speaking, but from listening to what is unsaid.
8. Nature has its own way of communicating, through stillness and silence.
9. Stillness allows us to process and absorb the lessons we have

learned.

10. Sometimes, the most profound stories are those that cannot be spoken aloud.

Chapter 17: The Weaver of Dreams

After leaving the Silent Forest, Lena traveled for several days through rolling hills and open plains, her heart still filled with the quiet wisdom she had gained from the forest's stillness. She reflected often on the lessons she had learned there, letting the silence guide her as she continued her journey. But as peaceful as the silence was, Lena knew that her journey would soon lead her to new discoveries, and the world would once again speak to her in ways that would challenge her to grow.

It was during this time of reflection that Lena heard of another place—a village hidden deep within the hills, where it was said that a mysterious woman lived who could weave dreams into cloth. The villagers called her the Weaver of Dreams, and her tapestries were said to hold the power to reveal one's deepest desires, fears, and hopes. Some said that those who visited her and gazed upon her work left changed, their lives forever altered by the visions they had seen.

The idea intrigued Lena. She had learned so much already, but the thought of seeing her own dreams and fears laid out before her was both exciting and terrifying. What would she see? What hidden truths would the Weaver's tapestries reveal? Lena knew that she had to find out.

The journey to the village was not an easy one. The path wound through narrow mountain passes and dense forests, and more than once Lena found herself wondering if she had taken a wrong turn. But just as doubt began to creep into her mind, she spotted the village nestled in a valley below, its rooftops barely visible through the thick trees.

As Lena entered the village, she felt a strange sense of calm settle over her. The air here was different—softer, almost dreamlike, as if the entire village existed on the edge of reality. The people moved slowly, their voices hushed, and there was a sense of reverence in the air, as if they were all aware of the power that resided in their midst.

Lena asked one of the villagers where she could find the Weaver of Dreams, and they pointed her toward a small cottage at the edge of the village, surrounded by trees and ivy. The cottage was unassuming, its walls made of stone and its roof covered in moss, but there was something about it that drew Lena in.

She knocked softly on the door, and after a moment, it creaked open. A woman stood in the doorway, her hair long and silver, her eyes bright and knowing. She was older than Lena had expected, but there was a lightness in her step and a warmth in her gaze that made her feel instantly at ease.

"You've come to see the tapestries," the woman said, her voice gentle but firm.

Lena nodded. "Yes, I've heard stories about them. They say your tapestries reveal things that people don't even know about themselves."

The woman smiled faintly, stepping aside to let Lena in. "Come," she said. "I am called Althea, and I weave not just with thread, but with the dreams of those who seek me. The tapestries do not lie, but they show only what you are ready to see."

Lena stepped into the cottage, her eyes drawn immediately to the large loom in the corner of the room. It was made of dark wood, its frame sturdy and polished, and stretched across it was a half-finished tapestry, its colors swirling together in intricate patterns that seemed to shimmer and move in the light.

"All dreams are made of threads," Althea said, her hands moving deftly over the loom as she spoke. "They weave through our minds, connecting our deepest desires with our greatest fears. My tapestries reveal those threads, and in doing so, they help people see what they have hidden from themselves."

Lena felt a mixture of excitement and trepidation. She had faced many challenges on her journey, but the thought of confronting her own dreams and fears in such a direct way made her feel vulnerable. But she knew that this was part of her journey—part of discovering who she truly was.

"Will you show me mine?" Lena asked quietly.

Althea nodded, her eyes never leaving the loom. "Yes," she said softly. "But remember—what you see is not the future, nor is it set in stone. It is merely a reflection of the threads that make up your life, the choices you have made, and the paths that lie before you."

With that, Althea began to weave. Her hands moved with a fluid grace, the shuttle gliding back and forth across the loom, the threads coming together to form patterns that seemed to shift and change with each passing moment. As Lena watched, the colors of the tapestry grew more vivid—deep blues, rich golds, and soft greens blending together in a dance of light and shadow.

The longer Lena watched, the more she felt herself being drawn into the tapestry. It was as if the colors were alive, moving not just across the loom, but through her mind, pulling at the edges of her consciousness. She saw flashes of memories—her home in Eldena, the stories she had heard as a child, the faces of the people she had met on her journey.

And then, slowly, the images in the tapestry began to take shape. Lena saw herself standing at a crossroads, the paths before her winding off into the distance, each one leading to a different future. On one path, she saw herself returning to Eldena, sharing the stories she had collected with her village, helping them see the world beyond their borders. On another, she saw herself continuing her travels, journeying to lands even farther than she had ever imagined, discovering new stories and new ways of life.

But there was more. The tapestry also revealed her fears—her fear of failure, of not being able to live up to the expectations she had placed on herself. She saw moments of doubt, of loneliness, of wondering whether she had made the right choices. And yet, woven through it all was a thread of hope—a golden thread that connected every part of her journey, reminding her that no matter where she went or what she faced, she was never truly alone.

Lena felt tears prick at the corners of her eyes as she gazed at the tapestry. It was beautiful, but it was also raw and honest, showing her not just the parts of herself she was proud of, but the parts she had kept hidden, even from herself.

Althea stepped back from the loom, her eyes soft as she looked at Lena. "This is your tapestry," she said quietly. "It shows the paths you have walked, and the paths that lie ahead. But remember, it is up to you to choose which path to take. The threads are yours to weave."

Lena nodded, her heart full of gratitude. The tapestry had shown her not just her dreams and fears, but the strength she had gained from her journey. It reminded her that every choice she made, every step she took, was part of the story she was creating.

As she left the cottage, Lena felt a sense of peace settle over her. She had seen her dreams laid out before her, and though the path ahead was still uncertain, she knew that she had the power to shape her own destiny. The Weaver of Dreams had shown her that the future was not something to be feared—it was something to be embraced, with all its possibilities and challenges.

The village of the Weaver of Dreams faded into the distance as Lena continued her journey, but the lessons she had learned there stayed with her. She knew that the road ahead would not always be easy, but she also knew that she had the strength and the wisdom to face whatever came her way. The tapestry of her life was still being woven, and she was ready to take control of the threads.

Lessons Learned

1. Dreams and fears are both important parts of our journey.
2. The future is not set in stone—it is shaped by the choices we make.

3. We all have the power to weave our own destiny, even when the path is uncertain.
4. Facing our fears can help us understand ourselves more deeply.
5. Reflection allows us to see the patterns in our lives and the choices that have led us to where we are.
6. Hope is a thread that connects all parts of our journey, even in difficult times.
7. We are never truly alone on our journey—our experiences and connections guide us.
8. Every person's life is like a tapestry, made up of the threads of their experiences, dreams, and choices.
9. Vulnerability is a strength—it allows us to confront the truths about ourselves.
10. The journey is ongoing, and each step we take brings us closer to understanding who we truly are.

Chapter 18: The People of the Tides

Lena's journey took her from valleys to mountains, from cities of invention to villages where dreams wove stories into reality. As she continued her travels, she realized that each place she visited gave her a new perspective on life, on the world, and on herself. But as much as she had learned, she knew that there was always more to discover, more stories waiting to be heard.

It was on a bright morning, with the sun shining high in the sky, that Lena found herself standing at the edge of the ocean for the first time. The vast expanse of water stretched out before her, endless and shimmering in the light. Waves crashed against the shore in a steady rhythm, their sound both powerful and calming. The ocean was alive, breathing with the rise and fall of the tides, and Lena felt a sense of awe wash over her.

She had heard stories of the ocean, of course—stories of great ships and distant lands across the water, of creatures that lived deep beneath the waves. But standing here, with the sea breeze in her hair and the salty scent of the ocean filling the air, Lena felt as though she were seeing the world for the first time.

As she walked along the shoreline, her feet sinking into the soft sand, Lena noticed a village in the distance. The houses were built close to the water, their wooden frames weathered by the salty air. Nets hung drying in the sun, and boats bobbed gently in the harbor. It was a small, quiet village, but there was something about it that drew Lena in.

When she arrived, the villagers greeted her with smiles, their faces tanned by the sun and their hands rough from years of working the sea. They spoke to her in warm tones, welcoming her to their village as if she were a long-lost friend. Lena felt an immediate sense of belonging here, as though the rhythm of the ocean had already woven her into the fabric of the village.

One of the villagers, a woman named Maris, offered to show Lena around. As they walked through the village, Maris spoke of the sea with reverence, explaining how the tides governed their lives.

"We live by the tides," Maris said, her voice soft but steady. "The ocean gives us everything we need—food, water, even the wood for our boats. But it also takes. The tides are powerful, and we must respect them. If we do not, we risk losing everything."

Lena listened intently, her eyes scanning the horizon where the ocean met the sky. She could feel the pull of the tides, the way the water seemed to move with a purpose all its own. It was both beautiful and terrifying, a reminder of the power of nature and the delicate balance that the villagers had learned to live with.

As they continued their walk, Maris brought Lena to a large stone at the edge of the village, where the waves lapped gently against its base. The stone was covered in carvings—intricate patterns and symbols that seemed to tell a story.

"This is the Stone of the Tides," Maris explained, her fingers tracing the carvings. "It has stood here for as long as anyone can remember. It tells the story of our people, of how we learned to live in harmony with the ocean."

Lena studied the carvings closely, her fingers brushing against the cool surface of the stone. The images were beautiful—depictions of waves, boats, and fish, interwoven with symbols that seemed to represent the sun, the moon, and the stars. But there was one carving that caught her attention more than the others—a figure standing on the shore, arms outstretched toward the sea.

"Who is this?" Lena asked, pointing to the figure.

Maris smiled. "That is the Tidekeeper. According to our legends, the Tidekeeper was the one who first learned how to read the tides. She understood the rhythm of the ocean, the way it ebbed and flowed with the pull of the moon. She taught our people how to build our boats, how to fish, and how to respect the sea. It is because of her that we have survived for so many generations."

Lena felt a sense of wonder as she gazed at the carving. The Tidekeeper was more than just a figure from legend—she was a symbol of the villagers' connection to the ocean, a reminder that their way of life was built on understanding and respect for the natural world.

As the sun began to set, casting a golden glow over the village, Maris invited Lena to join the villagers for their evening ritual. Every night, as the tide came in, the villagers gathered by the shore to watch the ocean, offering a quiet prayer of thanks for the gifts the sea had given them that day.

Lena sat with the villagers, her eyes fixed on the horizon as the waves rolled in, one after another. There was a sense of peace here, a feeling of being in harmony with the world. The villagers spoke in hushed tones, their voices blending with the sound of the waves, and Lena realized that this was more than just a ritual—it was a way of life. The ocean wasn't just a resource for the villagers; it was a partner, a living force that shaped their existence.

After the ritual, as the stars began to appear in the sky, Maris turned to Lena with a thoughtful expression. "You've traveled far, haven't you?" she asked, her voice gentle.

Lena nodded. "Yes, I've been to many places, and I've learned so much. But this place... it feels different. The way you live here, so connected to the ocean, it's beautiful."

Maris smiled softly. "The ocean teaches us many things. It teaches us patience, for the tides come and go in their own time. It teaches us respect, for its power is greater than anything we can imagine. And it teaches us to live in balance, to take only what we need and to give back whenever we can." Lena thought about Maris's words, letting them sink in. She had seen many different ways of life on her journey, but the people of the tides seemed to live in a harmony that was rare. Their connection to the ocean wasn't just practical—it was spiritual, a deep understanding of the rhythms of the world around them.

As the night wore on, Lena found herself reflecting on the lessons she had learned from the villagers. They had shown her that living in harmony with nature wasn't just about survival—it was about respect, about recognizing the interconnectedness of all things. The tides governed their lives, but in return, they had found a way to live that was sustainable, peaceful, and full of gratitude.

The next morning, as Lena prepared to leave the village, Maris presented her with a small gift—a smooth, round stone that had been polished by the ocean's waves. "This is a tide stone," Maris explained. "It's a reminder of the ocean's power and its wisdom. Carry it with you, and remember the lessons of the tides."

Lena accepted the stone with a grateful heart, knowing that it would be a symbol of everything she had learned in the village. The people of the tides had shown her a way of life that was deeply connected to the natural world, and as she continued her journey, she knew that the lessons of the ocean would stay with her.

Lessons Learned

1. Living in harmony with nature requires patience, respect, and understanding.
2. The natural world operates in rhythms, and learning to move with them can bring peace and balance.
3. Respecting the power of nature is essential to living a sustainable life.
4. Every part of nature, from the tides to the trees, is interconnected, and we are part of that connection.
5. Rituals can help us stay grounded in the present and connected to the world around us.
6. The ocean teaches us patience, as its rhythms are beyond our control.

7. Taking only what we need from nature ensures that future generations can thrive.
8. Living in harmony with the world around us brings a sense of peace and fulfillment.
9. The stories of our ancestors can guide us in living wisely with the earth.
10. The gifts of the natural world are meant to be cherished, respected, and shared.

Chapter 19: The Sky People

Lena's journey had taken her to villages tucked between mountains, hidden in forests, and resting beside the ocean. Each place had offered her a unique lesson about life, about balance, and about the interconnectedness of all things. But as she continued her travels, she found herself drawn to the sky—its vastness, its endless expanse, and the way it seemed to stretch beyond the boundaries of the earth.

The sky had always fascinated Lena. As a child, she would spend hours lying in the fields near Eldena, watching the clouds drift lazily across the sky, imagining what lay beyond them. Now, as she ventured farther from home, the sky became a constant companion, a reminder that no matter how far she traveled, the world was much larger than she could ever fully understand.

It was during one of these quiet moments, when Lena was gazing up at the sky, that she heard of a place where the people lived not on the land, but in the sky itself. The Sky People, as they were called, were said to dwell in floating villages, suspended high above the ground. They moved with the winds, their homes drifting on the breeze like clouds. It was said that they could read the skies, predicting weather patterns, storms, and even the movement of the stars.

Intrigued by the idea of a people who lived so close to the heavens, Lena set out to find them. The journey was long and difficult, taking her through rugged mountains and across vast plains. But eventually, Lena found herself standing at the edge of a great cliff, overlooking a valley far below. And there, in the distance, she saw them—floating villages, suspended in the air like islands in the sky.

The sight was breathtaking. The villages were made of light, delicate structures, their homes held aloft by large balloons and sails that caught the wind. Ropes and bridges connected the floating platforms, allowing the people to move between them. As Lena watched, she saw figures walking along the bridges, their movements graceful and sure, as if they had lived in the sky all their lives.

Determined to meet the Sky People, Lena made her way to a small path that led down the cliffside. It was a narrow, winding trail, but eventually, she reached the valley floor, where she found a group of Sky People preparing to lower a basket to the ground. The basket was attached to a long rope, which stretched up to one of the floating villages above.

Lena approached cautiously, unsure of how to introduce herself. But the Sky People, noticing her arrival, greeted her with warm smiles.

"You've come to see our village," one of them said, a young woman with windswept hair and eyes the color of the sky. "You're welcome to join us. The winds have brought you here, and we always trust the winds."

Lena smiled, grateful for the invitation. She climbed into the basket, her heart racing with excitement as the Sky People began to pull it up toward the village above. As the ground fell away beneath her, Lena felt a sense of awe wash over her. The earth seemed so far below, and the sky stretched out endlessly around her, vast and open.

When the basket reached the floating village, Lena stepped out onto the platform, her legs unsteady from the height. But the Sky People moved with ease, their steps light and sure as they walked along the wooden bridges that connected the different parts of the village.

The young woman who had welcomed Lena introduced herself as Aelith. She explained that the Sky People had lived in the sky for generations, learning to read the winds and the clouds, using their knowledge to navigate the changing weather patterns and keep their villages aloft.

"We follow the winds," Aelith said, her voice soft but steady. "The sky is our home, and we move with it. The clouds tell us where to go, and the stars guide us at night."

Lena listened in wonder, fascinated by the way the Sky People had learned to live in harmony with the sky. They didn't control the winds or the weather—they adapted to them, learning to move with the natural rhythms of the world above.

As Lena explored the village, she noticed that everything was designed to move with the wind. The houses were lightweight and flexible, their walls made of thin cloth that billowed in the breeze. The platforms were anchored to large balloons, which allowed them to rise and fall with the changing air currents. Even the people's clothing seemed to flow with the wind, light and airy, designed for life in the sky.

Lena spent the next few days living among the Sky People, learning their ways and listening to their stories. Aelith showed her how to read the clouds, explaining how different formations could predict storms or fair weather. She taught Lena how to navigate by the stars, using the constellations to find her way across the sky.

But it wasn't just the practical skills that fascinated Lena—it was the way the Sky People viewed the world. For them, the sky wasn't just a place to live; it was a source of wisdom, a guide that taught them how to move through life. They believed that the winds carried messages, that the clouds held secrets, and that by listening to the sky, they could find answers to their deepest questions.

One evening, as the sun set and the sky turned a deep shade of purple, Aelith invited Lena to sit with her on one of the highest platforms in the village. The air was cool and still, and the stars were beginning to appear overhead.

"There's something I want to show you," Aelith said, her voice barely above a whisper.

Lena watched as Aelith pointed to a cluster of stars near the horizon. At first, they looked like any other stars, but as Lena stared at them, she began to notice something different. The stars seemed to be moving, shifting ever so slightly, forming a pattern that was almost imperceptible.

"Do you see it?" Aelith asked, her eyes bright with excitement. "Those stars—they're part of a constellation that the Sky People have followed for generations. We call it the Wind Weaver. It appears only once every few years, and when it does, it guides us to new places, to new adventures."

Lena gazed at the constellation, her heart filled with wonder. The stars were beautiful, but more than that, they were a reminder of the vastness of the universe, of the endless possibilities that lay beyond the horizon.

Lessons Learned

1. Life is full of movement and change, and adapting to those changes brings peace.
2. The sky is a source of wisdom, and by observing it, we can find guidance in our lives.
3. Trusting in the natural rhythms of the world allows us to navigate challenges with grace.
4. The wind, the stars, and the clouds all hold messages if we learn to listen to them.
5. Flexibility and lightness help us move through life with ease, just as the Sky People's homes move with the wind.
6. The universe is vast and full of possibilities, and we are always part of its larger story.
7. Following the winds and stars can lead us to new adventures and discoveries.
8. The world has its own wisdom, and by learning from it, we can find harmony in our lives.
9. Life in harmony with the world around us brings a sense of peace and fulfillment.
10. No matter where we go, the sky is always above us, a reminder of the endless possibilities that await us.

Chapter 20: The Island of Forgotten Songs

Lena's journey continued, her mind and heart filled with the stories, lessons, and experiences she had gathered from the many places she had visited. Each village, each group of people, had its own rhythm, its own way of viewing the world, and each had shared something that left a lasting impression on her. Yet even with all the knowledge she had gained, Lena felt there were still new and untold stories waiting for her—stories that would help her understand the world even more deeply.

One such story was of a place called the Island of Forgotten Songs, a mysterious island shrouded in mist and legend. According to the tales, the island was home to songs that had been lost to time, melodies that had once been sung but had faded from memory. The people who lived there were said to be caretakers of these forgotten songs, preserving them in silence, waiting for someone to come who could bring them back to life.

Lena was intrigued by the idea of an island where songs were waiting to be rediscovered. Music had always been a part of her life, a way of expressing joy, sorrow, and everything in between. The thought of songs that had been forgotten, but still existed somewhere in the world, resonated deeply with her. She knew she had to find the island and learn its secrets.

The journey to the Island of Forgotten Songs was not an easy one. Lena had to sail across treacherous seas, navigating through dense fog that clung to the water like a veil. The waves were rough, and the wind howled around her, but Lena pressed on, her heart filled with determination. She knew that something important awaited her on the island, something that would help her understand the power of music and memory.

After several days of sailing, the island finally appeared on the horizon, its jagged cliffs rising out of the mist like ancient sentinels.

As Lena approached the shore, she could hear the faintest whisper of sound, like a melody carried on the wind. It was barely audible, more of a feeling than a sound, but it tugged at her heart, drawing her closer.

The island itself was quiet, almost eerily so. The trees swayed gently in the breeze, but there were no birds singing, no rustling of leaves. It was as if the island was holding its breath, waiting for something—or someone—to break the silence.

Lena wandered through the island's dense forests, her steps careful and deliberate. She knew that this place was special, that it held something precious, and she didn't want to disturb it carelessly. As she walked, she noticed that the trees were covered in strange carvings—symbols and patterns that seemed to form a kind of musical notation. It was as if the very trees were part of the forgotten songs, holding the notes and melodies within their bark.

After some time, Lena came upon a small village nestled in a clearing at the heart of the island. The houses were simple, built from wood and stone, but there was something serene and timeless about them. The people who lived there greeted her quietly, their eyes filled with warmth but their voices soft, as if they had grown accustomed to speaking in whispers.

Lena introduced herself and explained that she had come to learn about the forgotten songs. The villagers listened intently, nodding as she spoke, and then one of the elders—a woman with silver hair and a gentle smile—stepped forward.

"You have come to the right place," the elder said softly. "This island is home to songs that have been forgotten by the world, but they are not lost. They live here, in the silence, waiting for someone to give them voice again."

Lena's heart quickened. "How can I hear them?" she asked eagerly. "How can I bring them back?"

The elder smiled. "The songs are not gone, but they are hidden. They have become part of the island itself—part of the trees, the wind, and the earth. To hear them, you must listen with more than just your ears. You must open your heart, and the songs will find you."

Lena nodded, her curiosity piqued. She had always believed that music came from instruments, from voices lifted in song, but this was something different. The songs of the island weren't simply waiting to be played—they were woven into the very fabric of the place, like whispers of the past that needed to be uncovered.

That evening, as the sun set over the island and the sky turned shades of orange and pink, the villagers gathered around a fire. They didn't sing, nor did they speak much, but there was a deep sense of connection among them, as if they were sharing something unspoken. Lena sat with them, feeling the stillness of the island settle over her.

The elder approached Lena once again, this time holding a small, beautifully carved flute made from wood that glistened in the firelight. "This flute has been passed down through generations," the elder explained. "It was crafted to play the forgotten songs. But remember, the flute alone cannot summon the music. You must listen, feel the rhythm of the island, and let the songs come to you."

Lena accepted the flute with reverence, feeling the weight of its history in her hands. She closed her eyes, taking a deep breath as she let the sounds of the island wash over her—the whisper of the wind through the trees, the gentle lapping of the waves against the shore. It was all so quiet, but beneath the surface, Lena could feel something stirring.

Slowly, she lifted the flute to her lips and began to play. At first, the notes were hesitant, uncertain, as if she were searching for something just out of reach. But as she played, something shifted. The air around her seemed to change, and Lena felt the island itself begin to respond.

The notes flowed more smoothly now, weaving together into a melody that Lena didn't recognize, but somehow felt familiar. It was as if the song had been waiting for her all along, hidden in the silence, waiting to be brought back to life.

As Lena played, the villagers closed their eyes, swaying gently to the music. The song was soft, haunting, filled with a sense of longing and beauty. It spoke of things that had been lost, but not forgotten—of memories held in the heart, of love and hope that transcended time.

Lena played long into the night, the melody flowing through her like water. And as the song came to its gentle end, she felt a deep sense of peace settle over her. The forgotten songs had not been lost after all—they had simply been waiting for someone to listen, to bring them back into the world.

When Lena finally lowered the flute, the elder smiled at her, her eyes filled with gratitude. "You have done well," the elder said softly. "The songs were always here, but it takes a special heart to hear them. You have given them voice again, and for that, we are thankful."

Lena felt tears prick at the corners of her eyes, not out of sadness, but out of a deep, overwhelming sense of connection. The songs of the island had spoken to her in a way that words never could, reminding her of the power of music and memory, of the way that even things that seem forgotten can still live on.

The next morning, as Lena prepared to leave the island, the elder gave her the flute as a gift. "Take this with you," the elder said. "The songs of the island will always be with you, and wherever you go, you can share them with others."

Lena accepted the flute with a grateful heart, knowing that it would be a reminder of the lessons she had learned on the island. The Island of Forgotten Songs had shown her that music was more than just sound—it was a bridge between the past and the present, a way of connecting with memories, emotions, and stories that might otherwise be lost.

Lessons Learned

1. Music has the power to connect us to the past and the present.

2. Even things that seem forgotten can still live on if we take the time to listen.
3. Silence is not empty—it holds the potential for discovery and understanding.
4. We must open our hearts to truly hear the music that surrounds us.
5. Memories and emotions can be woven into music, telling stories that words cannot.
6. The simplest instruments can bring forth the most profound melodies.
7. Sometimes, the most powerful music comes from the quietest places.
8. Music can be a bridge between generations, connecting us to those who came before us.
9. Listening deeply can reveal hidden truths and forgotten stories.
10. We all have the power to bring forgotten things back to life, whether through music, memory, or love.

Chapter 21: The Desert of Hidden Paths

Lena had traveled through forests, mountains, villages, and islands, each offering her a new understanding of the world and herself. But as she continued her journey, she found herself drawn to a place that seemed more foreign than any other she had visited: the desert. It was a place of vast emptiness, where the wind swept across endless dunes of sand, and the sun blazed relentlessly in the sky. Yet despite its harshness, Lena had heard stories of people who lived in the desert, who had learned to thrive in a land where most would see only desolation.

The desert was known as the Desert of Hidden Paths, a place where travelers often lost their way, unable to see the paths that lay beneath the ever-shifting sands. But those who lived there—the Desert People—were said to possess a unique ability. They could see the hidden paths, the trails that the wind and sand covered from view, and they used this knowledge to navigate the desert with ease. Lena wanted to understand how they had learned to live in such an unforgiving place and what lessons they had to share.

The journey to the desert was long, the terrain changing gradually from grassy plains to rocky hills, and finally to the vast expanse of sand. As Lena stepped into the desert, the heat hit her immediately, the air dry and still. The sun hung high in the sky, casting sharp shadows on the dunes, and the wind carried the sound of nothingness, a silence that seemed to stretch out forever.

Lena walked for hours, her feet sinking into the soft sand with every step. The landscape seemed endless, the dunes rising and falling like waves frozen in time. She had been given directions to the village of the Desert People, but as she walked, she began to understand why the desert was called the Desert of Hidden Paths. There were no clear trails, no markers to guide her. The sand shifted constantly, erasing any footprints almost as soon as they were made. It was easy to feel lost in such a place, to feel as though the world had swallowed you whole.

But Lena pressed on, trusting in the stories she had heard, trusting that she would find the Desert People and learn their ways. As the sun began to sink lower in the sky, casting long shadows across the dunes, she finally saw it—a small village nestled at the base of a towering rock formation. The village was simple, made of tents and low stone buildings, but it was a welcome sight after the endless expanse of sand.

The people of the village greeted Lena warmly, their faces weathered by the sun but their eyes bright with kindness. They wore long robes to protect themselves from the sun's heat, and their movements were slow and deliberate, as if they had learned long ago how to conserve their energy in the harsh desert climate.

One of the elders, a man named Tahir, welcomed Lena to the village and offered her a place to rest. As they sat together in the shade of a tent, sipping cool water, Tahir began to explain the way of the desert.

"You've come to the Desert of Hidden Paths," Tahir said, his voice steady and calm. "Many travelers come here, thinking they can find their way through the desert by force of will alone. But the desert doesn't work that way. The paths are hidden for a reason, and only those who understand the desert can see them."

Lena listened carefully, intrigued by Tahir's words. "How do you see the paths?" she asked. "There's nothing but sand. How do you know where to go?"

Tahir smiled, his eyes glinting with the wisdom of someone who had spent a lifetime in the desert. "The paths aren't always visible," he explained. "But they're there. The desert has its own patterns, its own way of moving. The wind, the sand, the way the sun casts its light on the dunes—these are the signs we follow. We've learned to read the desert, to understand its language. And in doing so, we find the hidden paths."

Lena was fascinated. She had never thought of the desert as something that could be read, like a book or a map. But as she listened to Tahir, she began to see the desert in a new light. It wasn't just an empty wasteland—it was a place full of life and meaning, if you knew how to look.

The next day, Tahir offered to take Lena on a journey through the desert, to show her the hidden paths for herself. Lena eagerly agreed, excited to learn from someone who had mastered the ways of the desert.

As they walked together through the dunes, Tahir pointed out the subtle signs that guided him. The way a certain dune curved, the way the wind shifted the sand, even the patterns of the stars at night—all of these, Tahir explained, were part of the desert's language.

"It's not about forcing your way through the desert," Tahir said as they climbed a particularly tall dune. "It's about moving with it. The desert is always changing, always shifting. If you try to fight it, you'll get lost. But if you learn to move with the sand, to follow its rhythms, you'll find the paths that others can't see."

Lena followed Tahir's lead, watching closely as he navigated the seemingly featureless landscape with ease. She began to notice the patterns he spoke of—the way the wind moved the sand, the way the shadows shifted as the sun moved across the sky. It was as if the desert was alive, constantly in motion, constantly offering clues to those who knew how to look.

Lessons Learned

1. The paths we need to follow are not always visible, but they are there if we know how to look.
2. Patience and understanding are key to navigating life's challenges.
3. Moving with the natural rhythms of the world allows us to find our way more easily.

4. The desert, like life, is constantly changing, and we must learn to adapt to its shifts.
5. Trusting in the unseen can lead us to hidden opportunities and answers.
6. The landscape may seem barren, but it is full of life and meaning if we learn to see it.
7. Control is an illusion in the face of nature's power; it's better to move with the world than against it.
8. The wind, the stars, and the sand all have their own language, and by learning it, we can navigate even the toughest terrain.
9. Every environment, no matter how harsh, has its own beauty and wisdom.
10. Hidden paths, whether physical or metaphorical, are always there—we just have to learn how to find them.

Chapter 22: The Garden of Unseen Colors

Lena had walked through deserts, crossed mountains, and sailed across seas, learning and growing with each new place she encountered. But there was still a part of her that yearned to see something truly extraordinary, something that would challenge everything she thought she knew about the world. It was this desire that led her to seek out the Garden of Unseen Colors, a place spoken of only in whispers, where colors that had never been seen by human eyes were said to bloom.

The journey to the garden took Lena deep into a remote valley, surrounded by towering cliffs and dense forests. The air was thick with the scent of earth and flowers, but the path was overgrown and winding, as if the garden did not want to be easily found. She had been told that the garden was hidden from those who weren't ready to see it, that its secrets could only be unlocked by someone who was willing to look beyond the ordinary.

Lena's curiosity had always been her guide, and as she made her way through the valley, she felt it pulling her toward something unseen, something waiting just beyond the limits of her understanding. The landscape around her began to shift—trees grew taller, their trunks twisting in ways that seemed almost impossible, and the ground beneath her feet seemed to hum with life.

After what felt like hours of walking, Lena came to a clearing. In the center of the clearing stood a tall, iron gate, intricately carved with vines and flowers. Beyond the gate, Lena could see nothing but a shimmering haze, as if the air itself was alive with energy.

She reached out and touched the gate, feeling its cool surface under her fingers. The moment she did, the gate swung open silently, revealing the entrance to the Garden of Unseen Colors.

Lena stepped inside, her breath catching in her throat as she looked around. The garden was unlike anything she had ever seen. Flowers bloomed in every direction, their petals vibrant and alive, but there was something different about them. The colors—though beautiful—were not the colors Lena had known all her life. They shimmered and shifted, as if they existed in a spectrum that her eyes were only beginning to perceive.

It was as if the flowers were made of light itself, their hues constantly changing, moving from one shade to another in ways that defied description. Some of the colors were deep and rich, pulling at Lena's senses, while others were soft and gentle, almost whispering their presence.

Lena stood in awe, her heart racing with excitement. She had never imagined that such colors could exist. It was as if she had stepped into another world, one where the boundaries of what she understood about light, color, and vision had been completely rewritten.

As she wandered through the garden, Lena noticed something else—each flower seemed to carry with it a different feeling, a different emotion. Some filled her with joy, while others brought a deep sense of peace. There were flowers that made her feel as though she was floating, weightless and free, and others that grounded her, making her feel connected to the earth beneath her feet.

She reached out and gently touched one of the flowers, its petals soft and cool under her fingertips. The moment she made contact, a rush of warmth flooded through her, filling her with a sense of understanding she had never felt before. It was as if the flower had communicated something to her, not with words, but with color and sensation.

Lena closed her eyes, letting the feelings wash over her. She began to understand that the garden was not just a place of beauty—it was a place of deep meaning, where each color, each flower, carried with it a story, an emotion, or a truth that could only be understood by experiencing it.

The more time Lena spent in the garden, the more she realized that the colors were a reflection of something deeper, something unseen within herself. Each flower she touched brought forth a different part of her own journey—a memory, a lesson, or a moment of growth. The garden was showing her not just the world's unseen colors, but the unseen parts of her own heart and mind.

As the sun began to set, casting long shadows across the garden, Lena found herself standing in front of a large, brilliant flower, its petals glowing with a color she had never seen before. It was a deep, shifting hue that seemed to move between purple, blue, and green, but there was something more to it, something Lena couldn't quite describe.

She reached out, her hand trembling slightly, and touched the flower. The moment her fingers brushed its surface, a flood of images, feelings, and memories surged through her. She saw herself as a child, lying in the fields of Eldena, dreaming of far-off places. She saw her journey—the people she had met, the lessons she had learned, the stories she had gathered. And she saw the future—a path stretching out before her, filled with possibilities, with choices yet to be made.

The flower showed Lena that her journey was far from over, that there were still many more colors, many more stories waiting to be discovered. But it also reminded her that the journey was not just about seeing the world—it was about understanding herself, about learning to see the unseen parts of her own soul.

Lessons Learned

1. There are always new layers of beauty and understanding waiting to be discovered.
2. The unseen parts of the world often carry the deepest meaning.
3. Emotions and experiences are like colors—complex and constantly shifting.
4. True understanding comes from experiencing the world with

all of our senses, not just what we see.

5. Beauty can be found in unexpected places, beyond the limits of what we know.
6. Our inner selves are as rich and vibrant as the world around us, full of unseen potential.
7. The journey of self-discovery is as important as the journey through the world.
8. Colors, like emotions, cannot always be described in words—they must be felt.
9. Every experience adds a new layer to our understanding of ourselves.
10. There is always more to see, more to feel, and more to learn if we open ourselves to the possibilities.

Chapter 23: The Village of Mirrors

Lena's journey had taken her to places that challenged her understanding of the world, revealing unseen colors, hidden paths, and stories buried deep within the landscape. Yet there was one more place she had heard of in her travels, a place unlike any other—a village where the walls, houses, and streets were all made of mirrors. This village, it was said, was a place where people came to see themselves, not just as they appeared on the surface, but as they truly were, deep down inside.

The stories of the Village of Mirrors intrigued Lena. She had already learned so much about the world and herself, but the idea of a place that could reflect the innermost parts of a person, showing them truths they hadn't seen before, captivated her. She knew that whatever she found in the village would be difficult to face, but she felt ready.

The road to the Village of Mirrors was long and winding, cutting through forests and across rivers, but eventually, Lena saw it in the distance. The village shimmered in the sunlight, its surfaces catching the light and reflecting it in every direction. As she drew closer, Lena could see that the entire village was made of polished glass and mirrors, each surface reflecting the sky, the trees, and even Lena herself as she walked toward it.

Entering the village felt like stepping into a dream. Everywhere Lena looked, she saw her own reflection staring back at her. The buildings were tall and elegant, their walls made entirely of mirrors that seemed to stretch into infinity. The streets were smooth and gleaming, reflecting the sky above, and even the trees that lined the village had mirrors woven into their branches, creating a dazzling display of light.

Lena couldn't help but feel a little disoriented as she walked through the village. It was strange to see herself reflected from every angle, to catch glimpses of her face and body wherever she turned. But the people of the village moved with ease, seemingly unaffected by the constant reflections that surrounded them.

One of the villagers, an elderly man with kind eyes and a gentle smile, approached Lena as she wandered through the streets. "You're new here," he said, his voice soft but clear. "I can see it in the way you move. The Village of Mirrors takes some getting used to."

Lena nodded, her gaze shifting to the reflection of herself in the mirrored walls. "It's strange," she admitted. "Everywhere I look, I see myself."

The man chuckled softly. "Yes, that's the way of things here. The mirrors show us who we are, but not just on the surface. The longer you stay, the more you begin to see the parts of yourself that you've hidden away—the things you've buried, the things you've forgotten."

Lena's heart quickened at his words. "Is that why people come here? To see themselves more clearly?"

The man nodded. "Yes. The mirrors reflect more than just our appearances. They show us our fears, our desires, our regrets, and our hopes. They show us the truth, even when it's difficult to face."

Lena felt a flutter of anxiety in her chest. She had already learned so much about herself on her journey, but the thought of seeing her deepest fears and desires laid bare before her was unsettling. Yet she knew that this was part of her journey—part of understanding herself fully, without hiding from the things she didn't want to see.

The man gestured for Lena to follow him, leading her through the village to a quiet square at its center. In the middle of the square stood a large, circular structure made entirely of mirrors, its surface gleaming in the sunlight.

"This is the Mirror Hall," the man explained. "It's where people come to truly see themselves. The mirrors in this hall are different from the others—they reflect not just your body, but your mind, your heart, your soul. If you're ready, you can enter, and the mirrors will show you what you need to see."

Lena hesitated for a moment, her heart pounding in her chest. But she had come this far, and she knew that facing the truth was the only way to continue growing. She took a deep breath, then stepped forward and entered the Mirror Hall.

Inside, the air was cool and still, the light dim but steady. The walls were lined with mirrors, each one perfectly polished, reflecting Lena's image back at her from every angle. At first, she saw only herself—her face, her clothes, the way her hair fell over her shoulders. But as she stood there, staring at her reflection, something began to change.

The mirrors seemed to shift, their surfaces rippling like water. Lena's reflection blurred, and in its place, she saw scenes from her past—moments she had long forgotten, but that had shaped who she was. She saw herself as a child, playing in the fields near Eldena, her eyes filled with wonder as she dreamed of far-off lands. She saw herself saying goodbye to her parents before setting off on her journey, her heart filled with excitement and fear.

But then the scenes grew darker. Lena saw moments of doubt, moments where she had questioned herself, where she had felt lost and unsure of her path. She saw the times she had been afraid to take the next step, the times she had held back out of fear of failure. And deeper still, she saw the parts of herself she had tried to hide—the insecurities, the fears, the loneliness that sometimes crept in, even when she was surrounded by people.

Tears pricked at Lena's eyes as she watched the reflections play out before her. It was difficult to see, difficult to acknowledge the parts of herself that she had tried so hard to ignore. But the mirrors didn't lie. They showed her everything, even the things she didn't want to see.

But then, as the scenes continued to shift, Lena saw something else. She saw the strength she had gained on her journey—the resilience, the courage, the determination that had carried her through even the toughest moments. She saw the connections she had made with the people she had met, the way their stories had become a part of her own.

And she saw the love and joy that had always been there, even in the darkest times.

The mirrors were showing Lena the whole truth—not just the difficult parts, but the beautiful parts as well. They were showing her that she was not defined by her fears or her doubts, but by the choices she had made, the lessons she had learned, and the love she had given and received along the way.

Lena took a deep breath, her heart swelling with gratitude. The Mirror Hall had shown her everything—her past, her present, and even glimpses of her future. And while some of it had been painful to see, she knew that it was necessary. The truth was not something to be feared—it was something to embrace, something that would allow her to continue growing and evolving.

Lessons Learned

1. The truth about ourselves is not something to fear, but something to embrace.
2. We all carry both light and darkness within us, and acknowledging both is part of growth.
3. Mirrors—whether literal or metaphorical—can show us parts of ourselves that we've hidden away.
4. Facing our fears and insecurities is necessary for true self-understanding.
5. Our past, present, and future are interconnected, and each moment shapes who we are.
6. Strength and resilience come from acknowledging both our weaknesses and our strengths.
7. The difficult parts of our journey are just as important as the joyful ones.
8. We are more than our fears and doubts—we are also the love and joy we give and receive.
9. Self-reflection allows us to see ourselves more clearly and

move forward with purpose.

10. True growth comes from seeing ourselves as we truly are, and accepting all parts of our story.

Chapter 24: The City of Lanterns

Lena had journeyed through lands of beauty and mystery, through deserts, forests, villages, and islands that had each left their mark on her heart. She had learned from the people and places she visited, their stories weaving into her own. As her journey neared its end, Lena found herself drawn to one last place, a city she had heard whispers of since the beginning of her travels: the City of Lanterns.

The City of Lanterns was said to be a place where every story ever told was captured in light. The lanterns, which hung from every building and street corner, were more than just sources of illumination. They were symbols, holding within them the hopes, dreams, and experiences of those who had passed through the city. Some said that the lanterns themselves glowed with the essence of the stories they contained, their light growing brighter as the stories were shared and remembered.

Lena's heart swelled with anticipation as she approached the city. This was a place where stories lived on, where memories were preserved in a way that transcended time. For someone who had spent her entire journey gathering stories, the City of Lanterns seemed like the perfect place to reflect on everything she had learned.

As she entered the city, Lena was greeted by a sight that took her breath away. Lanterns hung everywhere—along the streets, from the rooftops, in the windows of houses and shops. They flickered gently in the evening breeze, casting a warm, golden glow over the city. Each lantern was unique, its light soft and inviting, as if beckoning passersby to pause and take notice.

The people of the city moved quietly through the streets, their faces peaceful, their eyes filled with a sense of reverence. It was clear that the lanterns meant something more to them than just light—they were guardians of the stories that had shaped their lives.

Lena wandered through the city in awe, her heart filled with a sense of wonder. She passed by a small shop where an elderly man sat outside, carefully tending to a lantern that flickered with a soft, steady glow. As she watched, the man adjusted the wick, ensuring that the light burned brightly.

"Is that your lantern?" Lena asked softly, curious about the story it held.

The man looked up and smiled. "It is," he said, his voice gentle. "This lantern holds the story of my family, the journey we've taken together, the love we've shared. Every night, I come out here to make sure the light is steady, so that our story can continue to shine."

Lena smiled, her heart warmed by the man's words. "That's beautiful," she said. "I've never seen anything like this before. The way the lanterns seem to hold something deeper than just light."

The man nodded, his gaze returning to the lantern. "That's the way of things here. Every lantern holds a story, and every story deserves to be remembered. Some are bright, filled with joy and laughter. Others are dim, touched by sorrow. But they all matter, and they all deserve to shine."

As Lena continued her walk through the city, she found herself wondering about the lanterns—about the stories they held and the people who had created them. She passed by lanterns that flickered with a soft glow, others that burned brightly, and a few that seemed to have gone out entirely, their light extinguished.

Curious, Lena approached a young woman who was sitting by one of the darkened lanterns, her face filled with quiet contemplation.

"Why isn't the lantern lit?" Lena asked gently.

The woman looked up, a small, sad smile on her lips. "It was my grandmother's lantern," she explained. "When she passed away, the light went out. I've been trying to decide whether I'm ready to light it again, to keep her story alive."

Lena felt a pang of empathy for the woman. "Do you think you'll light it?" she asked.

The woman hesitated, her eyes thoughtful. "I think so. I've been holding onto the grief of losing her, afraid that if I light the lantern again, I'll forget her. But I'm starting to realize that the light doesn't replace the person—it just helps keep their story alive. It's a way of remembering, of honoring what they meant to me."

Lena nodded, understanding the woman's feelings more deeply than she had expected. She had met many people on her journey, heard countless stories, and she knew how important it was to remember, to hold onto the lessons and the love that each story carried. The City of Lanterns wasn't just a place of light—it was a place of remembrance, where stories could live on even after the people who had told them were gone.

As the evening wore on, Lena made her way to the center of the city, where a large square was illuminated by hundreds of lanterns, their light casting a warm, golden glow over the gathering crowd. In the center of the square stood a tall, ornate lantern—larger than any Lena had seen so far. Its light was steady and bright, its glow reaching up toward the night sky.

Lena joined the crowd, her heart filled with a sense of anticipation. She could feel the weight of the stories around her, the collective memories of the people who had come before her, and she knew that this city was not just a place to visit—it was a place to leave something behind.

As the evening deepened, one of the city's elders stepped forward, his voice calm and steady as he addressed the crowd. "Tonight," he said, "we gather to light new lanterns, to bring new stories into the light. Each of us carries a story, a memory, a lesson that deserves to be shared. Tonight, we honor those stories and the light they bring to our lives."

Lena watched as people from the crowd stepped forward, each carrying a small lantern of their own. One by one, they lit their lanterns from the central flame, their faces filled with quiet reverence as the light spread through the square.

As Lena watched, her heart filled with a deep sense of gratitude. She had spent her journey gathering stories, learning from the people and places she had encountered. And now, here in the City of Lanterns, she realized that it was time to share her own.

With a steady breath, Lena stepped forward, her heart racing as she approached the central flame. She had no lantern of her own, but one of the elders handed her a small, simple lantern—a blank canvas, waiting to be filled with light.

Lena held the lantern in her hands, feeling the weight of her journey settle over her. She thought of the people she had met, the lessons she had learned, the love and the loss she had experienced along the way. She thought of her home in Eldena, of the storyteller who had first sparked her curiosity, of her parents who had watched her leave with both pride and worry in their hearts.

And then, with a deep sense of peace, Lena lit the lantern.

As the flame flickered to life, casting a soft, warm glow over her hands, Lena felt a rush of emotions—joy, gratitude, sorrow, and hope, all woven together into a single moment of clarity. This was her story, her journey, and it was time to let it shine.

Lena stepped back, watching as her lantern joined the others, its light merging with the collective glow of the city. It wasn't the brightest lantern, nor was it the dimmest, but it was hers, and it would continue to shine long after she had moved on.

As the night wore on and the lanterns filled the square with light, Lena stood in quiet reflection. She had come to the City of Lanterns seeking something—perhaps understanding, perhaps closure—but what she had found was something deeper. She had found a place where stories lived on, where the light of memory and experience could shine brightly, even in the darkest of times.

The City of Lanterns had taught Lena that stories were more than just words—they were light, they were life, and they were meant to be shared. And as she prepared to leave the city, she knew that her journey had come full circle. She had gathered stories, learned from them, and now she had shared her own, leaving a piece of herself behind to shine in the light of the lanterns.

Lessons Learned

1. Every story deserves to be remembered and shared.
2. The light of memory can keep our loved ones close, even after they are gone.
3. Stories have the power to connect us, weaving together the past, present, and future.
4. Grief and joy can coexist, and both are part of the stories we carry.
5. Sharing our own stories can bring peace and understanding to our journey.
6. Every life, every experience, has its own light that deserves to shine.
7. The stories of others enrich our own, adding depth and meaning to our journey.
8. We are never truly alone—our stories are part of a larger collective.
9. The act of remembering is a way of honoring the love and lessons of the past.
10. Stories are light—they guide us, inspire us, and continue to shine even in the darkest moments.

Chapter 25: Lena's Return

The road back to Eldena was long, but Lena's heart was light as she journeyed home. Her steps were steady, her mind full of the lessons she had learned, and her spirit carried the stories of all the places she had visited. Each story had shaped her, taught her something new about the world, and left its mark on her heart. But now, after so much time spent away, Lena knew it was time to return home and share what she had discovered.

As she approached the familiar hills that surrounded Eldena, Lena felt a surge of emotions rise within her. She had left her village so long ago, full of curiosity and wonder, eager to see the world beyond its borders. And now, she was returning as a different person—someone who had not only seen the world but had learned from it, someone who had grown in ways she couldn't have imagined when she first set out.

The sun was setting as Lena reached the outskirts of the village, casting a golden glow over the fields and houses. Everything looked just as she remembered, and yet, there was something different. Or perhaps it wasn't the village that had changed—perhaps it was Lena herself.

As she walked through the village streets, people began to notice her. Familiar faces turned toward her, eyes widening in recognition. Whispers spread through the village—Lena had returned.

Children who had once played by her side ran to greet her, their faces alight with excitement. "Lena! You're back!" they cried, their voices filled with joy. "Did you bring stories? Tell us what you saw!"

Lena smiled, her heart swelling with affection for the place she had always called home. "Yes," she said softly, "I brought stories—many stories. And I can't wait to share them with you."

As Lena made her way through the village, she saw her parents standing in the doorway of their house, their faces filled with emotion. Her mother's eyes sparkled with unshed tears, and her father's smile was both proud and relieved. Lena's heart clenched with love as she ran to them, wrapping them both in a tight embrace.

"You're home," her mother whispered, her voice thick with emotion. "You're finally home."

Lena nodded, her own eyes misting with tears. "I am," she said softly. "And I've brought so much with me—so much to share."

That evening, the village gathered in the central square, just as they had on the night Lena had first heard the traveling storyteller all those years ago. But this time, it was Lena who stood before them, ready to share the stories she had gathered on her journey.

The fire crackled in the center of the square, casting a warm glow over the faces of the villagers as they settled in to listen. Children sat cross-legged at Lena's feet, their eyes wide with anticipation. The adults, too, leaned forward, eager to hear what Lena had to say.

Lena took a deep breath, feeling the weight of the stories inside her, and then she began to speak. She told them of the places she had visited—the Village of Many Languages, the City of Inventors, the Island of Forgotten Songs, and so many more. She spoke of the people she had met, the lessons they had taught her, and the experiences that had changed her.

The villagers listened with rapt attention, their faces reflecting the wonder and awe of Lena's tales. They laughed at the story of the tiny elephant who had saved a village during a drought, and they grew quiet as Lena spoke of the wisdom of the Silent Forest. They marveled at the unseen colors of the Garden and the way the Sky People moved with the winds, and their hearts were touched by the stories of love and loss that Lena had gathered along the way.

But more than just the stories themselves, Lena shared the lessons she had learned—the importance of diversity, of seeing the world from different perspectives, of understanding that every person, every culture, had something valuable to offer. She spoke of the connections she had made, the kindness of strangers, and the power of stories to bring people together.

As Lena spoke, she could see the light of understanding in the eyes of her fellow villagers. They had spent generations telling the same story, but now, they were beginning to see that there were countless stories out there, each one as important and meaningful as the last. Lena's journey had opened their hearts and minds to the beauty of the wider world, and she knew that the stories she shared would continue to inspire them long after the night was over.

When Lena finished speaking, the village erupted in applause, their faces glowing with appreciation and admiration. Lena smiled, her heart full of warmth and gratitude. She had come full circle—she had left Eldena as a curious girl, and now she had returned as a storyteller, ready to share the lessons she had learned with the people she loved.

As the night wore on, the villagers gathered around Lena, asking questions, sharing their own thoughts and feelings about the stories she had told. The children begged her for more tales, and Lena promised them that there were always more stories to tell, more lessons to learn, more adventures to be had.

But it wasn't just the children who were eager to learn—Lena's parents, too, sat with her late into the night, their faces filled with pride as they listened to the tales of their daughter's journey. Her mother wiped away tears of joy, and her father's voice was thick with emotion as he said, "You've brought the world to us, Lena. We're so proud of you."

Lena's heart swelled with love for her parents, for the village that had raised her, and for the world that had taught her so much. She knew that her journey was far from over—there were always more stories to discover, more places to see—but for now, she was content to be home, surrounded by the people who had given her the courage to set out on her journey in the first place.

Lena had learned that every story mattered, that every person had something to teach, and that the world was a richer, more beautiful place because of its differences. And now, as she sat in the village square, surrounded by the people she loved, Lena knew that her own story was just beginning.

The world was full of stories waiting to be told, and Lena was ready to continue her journey, to keep learning, keep growing, and keep sharing the light of the stories she carried in her heart.

Lessons Learned

1. Every journey comes full circle, bringing us back to where we began, but with new understanding.
2. Stories have the power to open minds and hearts, connecting people across cultures and experiences.
3. Sharing what we've learned with others enriches their lives as well as our own.
4. The world is full of beauty, diversity, and wisdom, waiting to be discovered.
5. We are shaped by the stories we gather and the people we meet along the way.
6. Every place and every person has something valuable to offer, if we are willing to listen.
7. Home is not just a place—it's where our stories begin and where they can be shared.
8. The love and support of those around us give us the courage to explore the world.
9. Stories can inspire others to seek their own adventures and learn their own lessons.
10. The journey never truly ends—there are always more stories to discover, more lessons to learn, and more light to share.

The Good Child

Inspiring values and fellowship

About the Publisher

The Good Child Academy is a premier publisher dedicated to creating enchanting and educational children's books that inspire imagination and creativity. With a focus on delivering high-quality stories, the academy collaborates with talented authors and illustrators to produce books that captivate young minds. Specializing in themes like adventure, learning, and seasonal celebrations such as Halloween, Good Child Academy ensures that each book fosters curiosity, empathy, and a love for reading. Their mission is to nurture the next generation of lifelong readers.

Read more at https://www.patreon.com/thegoodchild/shop.